never kiss a stranger

winter renshaw

legal stuff

COVER DESIGN: Louisa Maggio @ LM Creations

INTERIOR FORMATTING: P.K. Culpepper

EDITING: Wyrmwood Editing

dedication

For Sadie.

also by winter renshaw

Coming soon!

connect

www.facebook.com/winterrenshawauthor

soundtrack

I've Been Thinking by Handsome Boy Modeling School

Coffee by Sylvan Esso

Waiting Line by Zero7

Soon We'll Be Found by Sia

Hard Road by Gia

Fading in C# by Ulla

As the Rush Comes by Motorcycle

Chemicals by Sirena

Arsonist's Lullaby by Hozier

Diet Mountain Dew by Lana del Rey

Big Girls Cry by Sia

Chelsea Hotel No 2 by Lana del Rey

Dark Paradise by Lana del Rey

Earned It by The Weeknd (Chrissy cover)

Thinking About You by Frank Ocean

table of contents

one

addison

Too pretty for a guy.

Swipe left.

Way too young.

Swipe left.

Not serious enough.

Swipe left.

Too serious.

Swipe left.

Reminds me of an ex.

Swipe left.

Hipster much?

Swipe left.

Oh. Hello.

Wilder. Age 27. 1 mile away. Active 24 hours ago.

I squeezed my eyes shut and reopened them, hoping that a fresh glance would help me decide whether or not I should swipe right on the guy with the impossibly kissable lips and Greek god nose wearing a tragically expensive suit in his profile pic. He was gorgeous. No, beautiful. A work of art if I'd ever seen one.

And it wasn't that I thought I deserved to be with someone who looked like him, nor did I even know if I someone like him would go for someone like me. But I'd be damned if I wasted my yearly one-night stand with a monkey-eared, buck-toothed, popped-collared, shaggy-haired, neighborhood frat boy. I'd evolved beyond that the year I graduated from college.

A deep breath passed through my lips as my fingers drummed across the back of my phone. An air of mystery seemed to surround him, most of which probably stemmed from the fact that his bio was blank.

My heart leapt as I stared at a man with whom I already had one thing in common: my bio was also blank.

The batteries of the meticulously clean vibrator hidden under folded Agent Provocateur panties in my top dresser drawer had long worn out, a sure sign that I was overdue for the real thing. It had been maybe a year since my last hook-up, which had consisted of a drunken hotel rendezvous with a rival real estate broker I had no business associating with in the first place. The next day, I barely remembered a thing about it besides the fact that I'd felt utterly and ridiculously unsatisfied with the entire encounter.

I licked my lips, moistening them after realizing my mouth had been hanging half open as I gawked at the stunning masterpiece in the photo. His navy suit could hardly contain his broad shoulders and a knowing smirk claimed his full lips. Not a strand of his thick, dark hair was out of place, cut low on the sides with a bit of length and a side part on top. I could only wonder what his voice might sound like if it vibrated low and throaty against my ears.

My eyes traced along the strong line of his half-clenched jaw, mentally picturing how it might flex when he was on the verge of release. Wilder appeared to be a man in control of his life. A man who knew how to have a good time. A man with intention and effort. A man who didn't have time for games and relationships, which was exactly the kind of guy I was looking for.

A warm tingle between my thighs told me my mind could waffle on him all night long, but my body had already made the decision for me. He was perfect, and he was perfect for me.

Swipe right.

I docked my phone on my alarm clock and pulled my freshly washed sheets up to my neck, rolling to my side. Five in the morning came early, and I rarely sacrificed a minute of sleep.

The traffic symphony outside my fifth-story window told me I was probably one of the only twenty-five year olds in all of Manhattan with a nine o'clock bedtime. I lived my life in numbers. Addresses. Purchase prices. Phone numbers. Meetings. Deadlines. Appointments. Important dates. My head spun most days, which left me drained with virtually no time for romantic relationships or so much as a trace of a sex life.

My phone buzzed just as I was about to nod off. Out of habit, I lunged for it. The whole city of Manhattan knew that an in-demand broker was never truly off the clock.

A little red icon over the dating app flashed bright in the darkness that filled my bedroom. The corner of my mouth slipped into a hopeful smile as blood rushed to my head. Could I really do this? Could I hit on a complete stranger on the Internet? Was I really this desperate?

My body begged and pleaded for me to just do it. Warmth spread between my legs. I needed to get laid. I needed to get it out of my system. This was what everyone was doing anymore, my assistant, Skylar, told me earlier in the day. She was maybe twenty-two with legs up to her eyeballs and a mess of satin blonde waves that hit right above the low-cut tops she always wore. If anyone knew how to get laid in this day and age, it was her.

I pressed the icon and a message popped up.

Hi, Addison. I'm Wilder. Can you talk?

My mind searched for something witty to say and came back empty-handed. It was too busy wrapping itself around the fact that this ridiculously gorgeous stranger had swiped right on my picture.

I'm awake, if that's what you're asking.

I cringed and deleted my message before I sent it. I couldn't tell him I was in bed. I didn't want to sound like a floozy, or worse, like I had no life.

Hi, Wilder. I can talk.

I sent the message and waited with bated breath for his response. Screw going to bed early. I couldn't possibly go to sleep now.

What's your number?

He wanted my number? What hot-blooded American man preferred talking over texting? My face fell. What if he was a lot older than he said he was? What if this was an old picture of him?

You want to talk on the phone?

A minute passed, and I feared the worse. He'd forgotten about me. Lost interest. Found me dreadfully boring or difficult. Decided the picture of me sitting on a friend's yacht in Cannes was too pretentious. I never should have used that picture. I wasn't normally so showy, but I worked hard for my lifestyle. I was proud, damn it.

212-555-7764. Call me now.

"Holy shit," I whispered out loud. I sucked in a deep breath as my thumb hovered over his number. Swallowing the lump in my throat, I practiced saying "hello" in my most sultry yet casual voice. I tapped his number and within seconds, the phone rang in my ear. I dealt with strangers all day, every day, but this was different.

"Hi, Addison." The deep purr of his voice had the potential to make me cream in my silk panties.

"Hi," I breathed. "Wilder. Is that your real name?"

"It is," he said with an amused huff.

"Not a fan of texting, I take it?"

"Hate it."

"You sure you're twenty-seven?"

"All right, Addison," he said. "You're not allowed to ask any more questions. Three's my limit."

My heart skipped a beat. "Fair enough."

"The only things you need to know about me are that I don't do relationships. I don't do labels. I don't do… emotions."

The corners of my mouth twisted into a grin I was thankful he couldn't see. He was perfect. I couldn't have chosen any better. "We have that in common, then."

"When can I see you?" he asked flatly.

The ache in my core longed to see him immediately. I needed him in the worst kind of way.

"Meet me tonight," he said, not giving me nearly enough time to decide.

"I work tomorrow. How about Saturday?"

"Saturday won't do. Tonight. One hour. W Hotel. Come as you are."

***

Am I really doing this?!

My heart drummed hard in my chest as I stood outside his room at the W Hotel on Lexington Avenue. Midtown wasn't my favorite place to stay, but I assumed he was trying to pick a centralized location having known virtually nothing about me.

I knocked lightly on the suite door. Staring down at my nude stilettos with crystal-covered heels and red soles, I tightened my cashmere blend trench coat around me. The soft fabric under my palm calmed my nerves, but only slightly. He told me to come as I was, but I'd have been damned if I was going to meet a man who looked like that and not dress myself to the nines. I smoothed a free hand over my loose, golden waves and quietly cleared my throat. My cheeks flushed at the thought that he was probably checking me out through the peephole as I stood there, waiting.

The moment the door pulled open, I wanted to throw up. Not in a bad way, but in an, "Oh, my God, he's so fucking gorgeous. What the hell does he want with someone like me?" way. Was this a joke, or did this guy not realize he could very well be the next Calvin Klein model covering a billboard in Times Square?

His aquamarine eyes studied me with an intensity that made my knees buckle.

"I knew you'd be lovely," he said. He held the door open and backed away, ushering me in with his sheer magnetism. He'd booked the best suite in the entire hotel, which was a nice touch, given the fact that this was simply a one-night stand. "Let me take that for you."

He reached for my coat, hanging it up in the closet behind the door.

"Are you normally this dolled up so late at night?" he asked, his eyes running the length of me and focusing on my blinged-out shoes. "I could have sworn I told you to come as you were."

I swallowed the lump in my throat and willed the heat rising in my cheeks to go the hell away as he stepped into my space.

"You're very pretty, Addison," he said. "You should know that."

I wanted to return the compliment, but I didn't want it to feel contrived, so I offered him a half-smile.

"Tell me why you're here," he said.

My brow twitched. "Isn't it obvious?"

He lifted a hand to my face and twirled a blonde wave around his fingers, letting the silky strand fall back onto my shoulder. "There are always two answers to every question: the one we tell ourselves, and the truth."

I stared up through mascara-covered lashes, my gaze landing on the hollow part of his cheek as his jaw subtly clenched. "I-I work a lot. I don't have time to date or meet men. I just wanted a release."

He pursed his full lips and cocked his head as his eyes scanned me once again. He removed the clutch from my hand and set it on a table. My eyes darted to it. I was very particular about my things, and I had to know where my phone was at all times. It was my lifeline. My job. My everything.

I didn't know what to do with my hands without something to hold onto. I glanced down at my fingers. The fuchsia paint on my left index finger was beginning to chip, and I had an intense urge to run straight home and fix it.

"Relax, Addison." His voice was like velvet fire as he leaned in and pressed his hot mouth into my flesh. He breathed me in as his hands went to my hips, digging into the dip of my hourglass frame. "God, you're tense. You always this tightly wound?"

"Excuse me?" I backed up, freeing myself from his clutches. "I am *not* tightly wound."

"Oh, believe me, you are. And you don't even realize it; that's the best part." His eyes held a mix of mischief and depth I'd never seen before. "You're a perfectionist. A control freak. You were shopping for a hook-up because you have very particular tastes. You don't settle. You seek… finer things. Not saying that I'm a fine thing—I'll let you be the judge of that. But I know what people see when they look at me. I know what I represent. And it's why I attract women like you."

I swallowed. He was reading me like a book, and I'd hadn't been around him for even five minutes.

"So, I believe your answer to my question, the reason why you're really here—the truth, if you will," he said, "is that you want to give up control. Temporarily, of course. But clinging so tightly to those regulations and routines has to be exhausting."

God, it was. But it made me feel safe. Being independent, making my own money, and working my ass off gave me security. And freedom. And only someone who'd been on the other side of all of that could appreciate it.

He reached for my hand, pulling me into him again. Our bodies pressed against each other, fitting perfectly like two fated pieces of a puzzle. He slowly raised his hand to my face, his fingers slipping through the hair at my nape and his thumb brushing against my jaw. "There's nothing more freeing than just letting it all go, Addison."

His mouth claimed mine.

That was quick.

It was weird kissing a stranger. I didn't feel a thing—at least, not in my head. The more I gave in to the moment, the more my body fueled a fire that'd been a year in the making.

When Wilder finally came up for air, his piercing eyes locked on mine. "What do you say? You ready to give up control for an hour of your painstakingly-perfected life?"

I nodded. It was why I was there. He had nailed it, and I couldn't deny how wonderful it sounded to let go.

Wilder's chocolate brown hair was tousled on top with a slight wave to it, matching his name and setting my curiosity afire. I hated that I couldn't read him the way he read me. I knew it was supposed to be a hook-up, a one-time thing, but how could I not want to know a little bit more about the man who had figured me out in all of three minutes?

His fingers worked my blouse one button at a time, and when he'd exposed the flesh of my bare stomach, he tugged the silky shirt off me and threw it on the floor.

"That's Rebecca Taylor," I said, staring at the crumpled designer, dry-clean-only top lying on the hotel carpet. He ignored me, already sliding my leather Prada leggings down my hips. He tugged my shoes off and threw each one in a different direction. I couldn't believe he could be so disrespectful to such beautiful works of art. I had worked my ass off to buy those. I'd come a long way from back-to-school shopping at Goodwill to running into Barneys and not even having to check the price tag on a pair of shoes.

Wilder cupped my face in his hands. The cool air of the hotel room enveloped my skin, prickling goosebumps on every square inch of me.

"They're only things," he said, studying my face. He stood waiting, his brows arched.

"Oh, yes," I said, realizing it was my turn to undress him. My cheeks flushed as I grabbed fistfuls of his navy blue sweater and tugged it over his hair, disheveling it even more. I ran my tongue across the fullness of my top lip as I worked his buttons and he loosened his tie, and within seconds, he was a shirtless vision of rippled abs and sculpted shoulders. He shoved his tie into his back pocket, and the second I reached for his belt buckle he stopped me, placing his hand over mine.

"This is where I take over," he said. "This is where you lose yourself in my world for the next hour."

The thought of giving up control both tantalized and terrified me. I quickly contained my fear, reminding myself of what I'd come there to do.

"Think you can do that, Addi?" he asked.

I groaned. "Please don't call me Addi. That's all I ask."

He frowned. "I call the shots here… *Addi.*"

I rolled my eyes.

"Fine," he said, leaning in and scooping his arm behind my waist. His lips found mine again and we stumbled back toward the bed. "I won't call you Addi. But everything else I might say or do tonight, lovely, is out of your control."

He laid me across the bed at an angle and lifted my arms above my head. Reaching into his back pocket, he pulled his silk tie back out and wrapped it a couple times around my wrists before securing it to the headboard.

I tugged at the straps that bound me. I was really tied up. This wasn't pretend. I pressed my lips together as my body tingled from head to toe and my clasped hands trembled.

As he hovered over me, the intensity of his raw verve drew attention to the burning desire in my core. He smelled like vetiver and cedar, tobacco and musk; like a rich cologne only a few fortunate individuals could afford to wear.

Wilder clicked off the lamp and lowered his body over mine. The floor-to-ceiling windows of our suite ushered in the flickering glow of New York City at night, and though we were amongst millions of people, we were in our own little world high above it all.

Wilder lowered himself to my hips, floating above my silk panties. His fingers slid beneath the waistband, traveling lower and pulling the fabric away from my mound.

"Exquisite," he said as he admired me. Red

bloomed in my cheeks, and I was thankful he couldn't see it in the dark. "Really. Exquisite."

And then he ripped them. My very expensive, French, silk panties. Ripped clean off me. I opened my mouth to protest.

"It's just a thing, lovely," he said again.

WILDER

She tasted of arousal with a hint of flowers, and I smiled at the notion that she'd spent time prepping for our little encounter. With her panties lying in shreds on the floor of the hotel suite, I devoured her intricately-groomed and deliciously sexy pussy.

My tongue separated her folds as I slid a finger inside her, previewing her warmth and wetness. She was tight, almost too tight, which matched her personality perfectly.

"Relax," I whispered. I glanced up to find her biting her tongue as her wrists wriggled and writhed against the tie the held them in place.

Soft moans escaped her full, fuckable lips, as if she were embarrassed to let herself go but couldn't fight it off completely. I breathed in her scent, letting it flood my lungs, and continued licking and exploring her beautiful pussy.

Had she been another girl, I'd have let her suck my cock and then finished myself off balls-deep inside her, but Addison was different. There was something about her that told me this probably wouldn't be the last time I saw her.

She needed me, whether she knew it or not.

I peeled myself away, leaving her panting and breathless and probably relieved to get a break from fighting off her orgasms for a minute, and searched for the foil packet I'd set on the nightstand earlier.

Sheathing my engorged cock, I readied myself at her wet and ready entrance. "Are you ready, lovely?"

She lifted her head toward me, her eyes seeming confused even in the dark. "I didn't realize this was going to happen so quickly,"

"Do you want more foreplay?" I asked. "I could let you suck my cock, but I'd much rather bury it deep inside this pretty little pussy of yours."

Her head fell back into the soft pillow and she nodded. "Do whatever you want to me, Wilder."

I wasn't a man whore by any stretch of the imagination, but most of the girls I'd been with were so fake in the sack it took everything I had to keep my dick hard. They'd enthusiastically suck my cock like it was a fucking lollipop and then scream out my name as if they were auditioning for a goddamned porno. Addison was real. All she did was be herself.

And it made me hard as fuck.

I pressed the head of my cock toward her soft entrance and inserted myself inch by inch until I was all the way in. She felt like heaven, like a teenage boy's wet dream and a night at the Playboy Mansion all rolled into one. If pussies came in luxury models, hers was the Rolls Royce. Tight and soft. Wet and inviting.

One thrust. Two thrusts. Slow at first, then building. Each thrust brought me closer to the brink, much to my dismay. I could last for hours in any other woman I'd bedded, but not Addison.

I forced myself to think of other things. Baseball. The stock market. Smog. But they kept coming back to her and how fucking amazing she felt on my dick. Her hips wriggled and bucked beneath me, meeting me thrust for thrust, and she gripped onto the tie each time I hit her wall.

"Wilder," she panted. "Oh, my God…"

My hand traveled up her breasts, a pert nipple tickling my palm, and then landed under her jaw. My thumb traced over her fuckable pink mouth. I'd have to know what it felt like another time.

I fucked her as long as I could, filling my mind with as many unsexy thoughts as I could in an attempt to stave off the inevitable. She bucked hard against me as sexy moans and expletives flew from her lips, so I had to correct her. "No, lovely. I'm in control."

"But I can't fight…" she breathed, her words trailing as she attempted to obey me.

"Trust me. I know what you need," I said in a low whisper.

I didn't want to pull out of her. I wanted to stay in her forever, bask myself in her musky arousal, fuck her all night long, round after round. I barely knew her, and yet she was one of the most fascinating people I'd ever met. I'd never met a girl so prim and proper and perfect who quietly preferred to be tied up and fucked like that. I supposed it made sense though.

Addison fought it long and hard, but after a while her body gave up the fight, practically convulsing as she bit her lip to keep from screaming. I released myself as she wriggled and bucked against my cock.

The second she caught her breath she glanced at the nightstand toward the alarm clock. "Shit. I have to go. I have to be up in six hours."

I raked my hand through my hair. "Seriously?"

She just came all over my cock, and that was the first thing she had to say when it was over and done with?

"Untie me," she said, immediately returning to pre-fuck Addison. I tugged on the strap of the tie, unraveling it. She rubbed her wrists and scooted off the bed while I enjoyed the view.

She was a true hourglass: curved hips, whittled waist, round, natural breasts. She could've given Marilyn Monroe a run for her money, back in the day. If I had to guess, she probably didn't know how sexy she was, or it was so removed from her perfect list of priorities that it didn't matter.

She rifled around the room, searching for the bits and pieces of the clothing she'd shown up in.

"You mind calling me a cab?" she asked as she grabbed a sparkling stiletto from the floor.

Women like her, the workaholic types, only gave their sexuality a thought when they realized how much their girlfriends were getting laid or when they were lying awake at night thinking about how good it would feel to have hot sex right about then. I imagined that was how Addison found me.

Admittedly, I was doing the same thing. Looking for a one-night stand. An innocent hook-up. A beautiful girl to bury my dick in for an hour or so. But now that I'd had her once, I wanted to have her again.

I pulled my jeans back on and flipped on the light. She was all dressed, save for the torn underwear lying on the ground.

She stepped toward me, as if she didn't know how to say goodbye.

"I've never done this before," she said, her eyes shifting nervously. "For the record."

"I figured."

"Thanks for tonight," she said in a low husk with the tiniest hint of a southern drawl. "I needed it."

Her pretty blue eyes washed over me, as if she wanted to get one last glance at me before she left. She wrapped her cream coat around her and secured it with a shiny, glass button. She looked just as beautiful leaving as she had when she'd arrived. The flush on her cheeks were the only sign that she'd just been fucked. Other than that, she was pure elegance.

"Look, lovely," I said, combing my fingers through the side of my hair. "I don't do relationships, or anything like that, but if you wanted this to be a regular thing, I could probably make that happen."

I couldn't believe I was propositioning her. It never happened this way. It was usually the girl pretending she wasn't interested in me, like I wouldn't know what reverse psychology was, and her subtly hinting about hanging out again.

Addison made no mention of seeing me again, and I suppose the fact that she could have very easily walked out of there that night and I'd have never seen her again made me break my rules.

Her full lips arched upward at the corners as her blue eyes glinted. "This was a one-time thing, remember?"

She walked to the door, seconds from walking out of my life forever. I couldn't let that happen.

I cut her off, placing my hand on the door. "Maybe I didn't make myself clear just a second ago."

"What's that?"

"I have to have you again."

three

addison

"Of course you want to be with me again," I said. "I just let you tie me up and have your way with me."

Wilder winced in pain—the emotional type, not the physical. I was quite positive most women threw themselves at him.

"I meant it when I said I don't do relationships," I said.

"I did too." His teal eyes searched mine. "I don't do relationships. Hooking up on a regular basis does not constitute a relationship, Addison. Not in my world."

"You say that now," I said, "but I know how these things happen. We'll hook up a few times. Maybe one night we'll be hungry, so we'll run out to get dinner. We'll inadvertently get to know each other, which will make us start caring about each other. We'll look forward to the next time we see each other again, and then we'll start having romantic thoughts."

He could argue his point all he wanted, but I knew I was right. I'd been down that road before. Besides, I was already in love.

With my job.

He scoffed. "I don't want to get to know you. I don't even know your last name. I'll never ask, I promise. And I won't tell you mine."

I stared at him. He really wanted me, and I couldn't deny how good it felt to be desired again. But still. I didn't have time for a relationship. That was why I hooked up with him in the first place.

"Why?" I asked. "You don't need me. There are millions of girls out there who'd kill to be your little sex toy."

One look into his eyes coupled with the things I knew he could do to me physically, meant I could very easily fall in love with him if I wasn't careful, and that was exactly why I had to nip it in the bud.

"I've met a lot of Nikkis," he said. "Nikkis are all bat-shit crazy. Sexy as fuck, but crazy. I've met Ashleys, Jennas, Tiffanys. Even a few Chloes. They're all the same. Pretty, yet shallow. Every single one of them. But I've never met an Addison. You're different, and you intrigue me."

"We could have the best intentions, Wilder, but we can't control the uncontrollable." I placed my hand on the doorknob. I breathed him in one last time. "If you'll excuse me, five a.m. comes early."

* * *

I skipped my run that next morning. I never did that. I'd had the best sleep of my entire life, courtesy of an earth-shattering orgasm. I was out like a rock.

"Shit." I popped out of bed, realizing my alarm had never gone off. If it had, I must have turned it off in my sleep. The sun was already out, which meant it was well past seven and I had less than an hour to put myself together and make it downtown to my office.

I took a quick shower and slipped into a navy pencil skirt with matching heels and a cream blouse, reminiscent of the one I'd worn to see Wilder the night before.

An hour later, I was running off the elevator toward my office.

"You okay?" My assistant, Skylar, watched me with big, brown eyes. "You're, like, never late."

She was right. I was never late. And the day I hired her, I told her that being ten minutes early to work was still considered late in my book. I'd written her up for being five minutes late before, but now I was going to have to cut her a little slack.

"Brenda wants to have a meeting with you and Kyle," she said.

"When?"

"Now." She pointed to the conference room where the door was slightly ajar.

I collected my thoughts and headed in.

Impromptu meetings between myself, my boss, Brenda, and my arch nemesis and biggest competitor, Kyle, were never a good thing. Kyle and I had dated for a couple years, but we'd always kept it under wraps. Brenda would have freaked out if she knew and demanded that one of us quit.

It couldn't be about that, could it?

I wasn't about to quit, though, and definitely not because I was all love-swept over that nitwit for two years of my life. I was having the best year ever, about to clear a couple of record breaking commissions, which would put me in the top 1% of real estate brokers in all of Manhattan. In a city with over thirty-thousand agents, Kyle and I were both in the top 1%, and Brenda Bliss of Bliss Agency was our boss.

We'd been under her umbrella for a few years, doing all the hard work and schmoozing and selling while she sat back in her expansive corner office and plastered her name on all the signs and billboards and accepted all the awards.

I'd been busy making connections the last few years, but my goal was to have a team of my own very soon, and someday maybe my own agency. My ultimate goal was to become the number-one realtor in the entire city. Last I checked, Kyle and I both teetered back and forth between the seventh and eight spots.

"Morning." I smoothed my pencil skirt under my thighs and took a seat across from them. They both stopped talking and stared at me as I sat down, as if I'd just interrupted a very important conversation. "What's this about?"

Brenda's thin red lips danced into an excited grin as her gaze alternated between us. Kyle's smirk and too-close proximity to Brenda instantly made my skin crawl. He was constantly pouring the charm on her, and I'd have killed to know if she saw through him. Part of me figured she lapped it up because she was a desperate woman who craved that sort of attention.

"We are courting a very high profile client," she said. She smelled of excitement, money, unbridled ambition, and greed. She'd get to sit back and steal the glory while we did all the hustling. "I can't tell you who it is, but he is wanting to interview two members of my team. My best. You two."

She placed one manicured hand over mine and the other over Kyle's. She was old enough to be our mother, and if she were, she'd have been the passive-aggressive, guilt-trip-inducing kind. Thank God she never had kids of her own.

"The meeting will be in two weeks," she said. "You're lunching at Butter. You'll each sell yourselves and he'll pick the person he feels will suit his needs best. I want you on your best behavior. Best clothing. Best presentation. A-game all the way."

"Always," Kyle said. I wanted to tell him to wipe the shit off his nose. Instead, I smiled.

"Do we know anything about him?" I asked.

"We know he's a major, up-and-coming Manhattan real estate investor," she said. "He has a lot of cash to spend and he wants to spend it quickly."

"Do we have a name?" Kyle asked.

She pursed her lips and shook her head. "His assistant kept referring to him as Mr. Van Cleef of Van Cleef Investments. I tried looking up his company. They have a website, but I didn't see anything about staff or an owner or anything. It's a new company, though, and if we can make him happy, we'll have a client for life. That's my motto, guys—you know that."

"Client for life!" Kyle jabbed his fist into the air triumphantly and Brenda smiled, only I knew he was half-mocking her.

He used to mock her all the time back when we were together, but I had enough wits about me not to badmouth my boss to the man I was sleeping with. He may have been ridiculously good-looking, like a walking talking J. Crew advertisement complete with a New England pedigree, but no one ever accused Kyle Maxwell of having common sense.

He raked his hand through his sandy blond hair and flashed his million-dollar smile at Brenda. His eyes, green and hazel like a fresh caramel apple, flashed with the kind of confidence he'd honed with years of practice. "Don't worry, Bren, we got this."

I cringed, remembering how charming I used to find him. Years ago, I was just a junior agent barely making a livable wage. Brenda took a chance on me and brought me on her team while Kyle took me under his wing. At first he treated me like a kid sister and called me "Addi." I'd always hated that nickname, but it was different when he said it.

"What would we do without our Kyle?" I said with an undercurrent of facetiousness as I folded my hands in my lap and sat up straight. I plastered the fakest smile I could muster across my face as Brenda giggled like a schoolgirl as if being in Kyle's mere presence was hilarious.

"Better bring it, Addi." Kyle spoke to me, but his eyes never left Brenda's. His left hand rested on the table, his titanium wedding band catching the glint of the late afternoon sun. I still couldn't believe he was married.

My mentorship with Kyle years back had evolved into a relationship lasting just under two years. Our splendor in the grass had come to a screeching halt when I discovered he was sleeping with a select handful of his client; one of which he eventually married. From what I heard, she was old enough to be his mother.

Kyle was a shameless cougar hunter, and I was nothing more than his beard. And to think, all those times he'd held me late at night and told me he loved me and called me "Addi," I'd thought I was in love.

Now he made me want to throw up a little in my mouth.

All I knew was that I never wanted to feel that way ever again, so I made a commitment to myself and to my job.

"All right, let's get to work, you two," Brenda said, winking at Kyle.

I hurried back to my office and fired up my

computer. My cell phone buzzed in my pocket with a vaguely familiar looking number.

"Hello?" I answered.

"Addison."

Oh, God, it was him. The voice that made me cream. I flew to my office door and practically slammed it shut. My heart raced and my face flushed as if the whole world knew what I'd done the night before.

"Why are you calling me, Wilder?" I whispered.

"Why are you whispering?" he whispered back, mocking me.

"I'm at work right now."

"So am I."

"Shouldn't you be working?"

"Don't you want to know why I'm calling?"

I did and I didn't. In my heart of hearts, I knew what he wanted. "I told you, I can't do whatever it is you want to do with me. It was a one-time thing."

"What can I say to change your mind?"

"I don't know. You seem to have me figured out pretty well. Why don't you think of something?"

"That's the thing," he said, his voice low and steady. "I can't figure you out, and it's driving me insane. I thought I had you pegged, but I realized after you left last night that I'd barely scratched the surface."

"See, you *do* want to get to know me," I said. "I know where this leads, Wilder, and I cannot go down this road. Not at this point in my life."

"I don't want to date you, Addison," he said. "I want to own your body. There's a difference."

His voice came to growl over the mention of the word "own," and it made me shiver. I swallowed the lump in my throat, but it returned as quickly as it'd left. My life was stressful, and Wilder could provide a temporarily relief from that.

"Let me think about it," I sighed, my heart swinging between clinging onto my polished and controlled way of life or running into the arms of the exciting unknown.

I ended the call with Wilder just as an email popped up from my sister.

Don't forget. Dinner reservations tonight at CRAVE. 7pm. Don't be late this time!

xoxo,

Coco

I checked my schedule to make sure I didn't have any showings that night, and fired back a response letting her know I'd be there. On time. She was such a mother hen sometimes, but it was only fitting given our background. She'd pretty much raised me when our mother, Tammy Lynn, spent most nights at the bar or going home with strange men. Coco was only two years older than me, but she always made sure I was fed and clean and got to school on time.

* * *

"I got here first," I said in a singsong voice as Coco arrived at our table that night. It was pure luck, though. I had a showing that ran later than expected, but I'd hailed a cab and slipped him an extra twenty to drive like a maniac so I'd get there first.

"Miracles do happen," Coco teased, setting her jet-black Hermes bag on the empty chair between us. Dark waves like spun silk rested over her the shoulders of her tweed Chanel jacket and spilled down her back, and I quietly envied the fact that rain, snow, or shine, she always looked like a million bucks. Of course it was just part of her job as a weekend morning anchor for the highest-rated news network in the country. She always had to be on.

The restaurant was packed. Coco always picked the hottest places.

"Miss Bissett, I'm sorry to bother you," a middle-aged woman said as she approached our table. "Can I get a picture with you?"

Coco happily obliged and stood up as the woman handed me her phone. I was always the picture taker, but I was used to it. I was damn proud of my big sister. We'd both risen from nothing. Who knew two girls from a trailer park in Darlington, Kentucky could move to Manhattan and make something of themselves?

The woman scampered away, staring at the screen of her phone, happy as a clam, and Coco took a seat again.

"You're so nice, Co," I said, shaking my head.

Less than ten years ago, Coco Bissett was an unknown aspiring broadcast journalist named Dakota Andrews. She'd married well in her early twenties to a prominent Manhattan man named Harrison Bissett, who happened to be about ten years older than she was. Harrison also happened to be a producer for a news show on MBC, which meant he had a whole host of highly coveted connections. It wasn't long before she kicked her Kentucky accent to the curb and worked one on one with a hosting coach. Shortly after that, she was doing screen tests and fill-ins and the offers began to pour in.

When she landed the weekend morning show, Harrison insisted Coco Bissett sounded more commercial and like a name that would give her more credibility than Dakota Andrews. It was weird thinking of her as anyone other than Coco Bissett anymore, and it was almost as if Dakota Andrews never existed in the first place.

We'd come a long way from crawling around on dirty floors to clicking our Manolos across the marble of some of the most expensive apartment homes in the whole world.

"It's all part of the job, Addison," she said anytime I questioned anything.

We each had our own forms of validation. Mine came in the form of signed contracts and six-figure commission checks. Hers came in the form of being loved and adored by complete strangers.

"Did you hear the big news?" Coco asked as she sipped her Perrier. Her big blue eyes, which matched mine right down to the icy gray flints in our irises, twinkled against the flicker of the candlelight.

"No?"

"Mom's getting married."

"Again? What is this, number six?"

"Five. I think. If we're not counting Dale."

"Oh, God, let's not count Dale." I shuddered to think of the hairy man who compulsively lied to our mother and swindled her out of what remained in her pitiful 401k. Coco and I would be taking care of Mom someday, we knew it, but at least we'd always planned for that. The worst part was Dale insisted they be common law married because he was all tied up in a long, ongoing divorce to a woman in Iowa. We found out that woman never existed, and it was all just a scam. He was one of *those*. "What's his name?"

"Does it even matter?" Coco rolled her eyes and then plastered her best made-for-TV smile as soon as our server approached us. She controlled her emotions with a switch. "Yes, hi, I'd like a glass of pinot noir, please. Thank you."

"Gin and tonic for me, thanks," I said. "So, when is Mom planning on telling me?"

"I don't know. Soon," Coco said. "She just told me today. She and her new husband-to-be are coming to the city. I guess he has a son who lives here. She wants us all to do dinner."

"One big, happy family."

"Exactly." Coco took a sip of her freshly-delivered wine. "That woman is persistent. She's fifty-eight years old and won't give up on the notion that we need to have this perfect nuclear family."

"That ship has sailed."

"You're tellin' me," Coco said, and a hint of the Kentucky accent we'd both buried years ago came out to play. When we first moved to New York, we'd practiced for months at hiding it, and Coco had learned a few techniques in college when she studied broadcast journalism. No one could tell we were from Kentucky anymore, though occasionally when one of us got mad, the accent came out in full force.

Coco's phone began to vibrate, and she raised a finger and mumbled an apology as she answered the call. It was probably Harrison. Her ex-husband. I never understood their relationship, and Coco would never elaborate too much about why they had been divorced for two years but still lived together.

"You just want me to move so you can sell me an apartment," she'd tease, trying to change the subject.

Coco wandered off from the table to take her call, and from the looks of her flailing hand motions, she and Harrison were going at it again. My sister was fiercely independent, but she loved just as hard as she lived her life, and her tender heart was her Achilles heel.

Which was also why we were never allowed to talk about her high school boyfriend who was now a famous country music singer. Never mind the fact that his face was plastered over every billboard in Times Square every time one of his albums came out. She seemed to live her life like he never existed, and I'd feel her wrath if I dared mention his name or his music around her.

I took a sip of my cocktail as I waited and rearranged my silverware, scanning the room for a familiar face. I'd sold and leased thousands of apartments and condos and brownstones over the last few years, and I always seemed to run into people I knew anytime I was out. It had become something of a game for me.

As I glanced around, I filled my mouth with another sip of my drink, practically choking as soon as I saw him.

Wilder.

At this restaurant.

Sitting across from a woman with blonde hair like mine.

And he saw me.

I coughed as the sip slid down the wrong pipe, bringing a linen napkin to my lips as I tried to get it under control. I wedged myself out and away from the table and headed toward the bathroom, not wanting to make a spectacle of myself.

I'd forced him out of my mind that day so I could get a little work done, and I still hadn't decided what I was going to do about him. There was no denying how liberating it was to give up control of my body to a man who knew exactly what to do with it. But there was also no denying how freeing it was to have total possession of my own heart.

When I emerged from the bathroom, he was standing there. Arms crossed. Smirk across his face. Waiting for me.

"Small world," he said, looking me up and down.

He stepped into my space, owning it. "You here on a date?"

"No," I said. "My sister. She's around here somewhere. You?"

"Here with my aunt. Definitely not a date," he said. "I'm a kinky man, lovely, but I'm not that kinky."

"Okay, well, enjoy your dinner," I said, trying to play coy and hoping he couldn't see the effect he was having on me. Being in his presence made it hard to breathe, and I could barely think straight when we locked eyes.

"Wait," he said. His hand took my wrist and guided me back to him. "Is this how you dress when you're having dinner with your sister?"

He glanced down at my blouse. A few of the buttons had come undone throughout the day due to stretched button holes. I'd been meaning to take it to a tailor, but I'd been too busy lately. His hands gripped the side of my hips as he ran them down the smooth fabric of my hip-hugging pencil skirt.

"What's wrong with what I'm wearing?" I asked him.

His determined hands slid up to the curve above

my hips, and he stepped closer to me until his body had nearly pinned me against the wall. He leaned down, his lips against my ear, and said, "Because this sexy little body of yours belongs to me, and you're showing it off for the rest of the world."

His voice vibrated low and tickled my eardrum, sending my heart into instant arrhythmia.

"I don't like to share," he said. "That's another thing you should know about me."

My words caught in my throat as my thoughts scrambled in every direction. I couldn't possibly have casual sex with a man who made my body betray my mind the way Wilder did. He could be very bad for business. He could wreak all kinds of havoc with my priorities. My life's work. And I couldn't afford to cheat on my work with a plaything like him.

"I still haven't given you my answer," I said. "Aren't we getting a little ahead of ourselves?"

"Look," he said. "We both know how this is going to go. I won't take no for an answer, and you're going to give into me sooner or later once you realize I'm exactly what you need. Let's drop this little act of yours and stop wasting each other's time."

He leaned in and placed a single, tantalizing kiss on my lips as if to intentionally tease me.

"Why me?" I asked.

"Why not you?" he huffed, as if it were obvious. "We're perfect for each other. Can't you see that? We're not looking for love or a relationship. You're looking for a man to take complete control of you behind closed doors, to make you forget about this crazy, busy, ridiculously over-controlled life you're living, and I'm looking for a beautiful woman who likes to hand over the reins in bed. You have what I need. I have what you need. It's that simple, lovely. Don't make it complicated."

"Addison, you okay?" It was Coco. I peered from around Wilder's broad shoulder to find her standing there with her hand on her hip, watching this wildly attractive man in a three-piece suit press me up against a wall.

My cheeks burned red with embarrassment. "I'm fine." I pushed myself away from Wilder and shooed Coco away as I straightened my blouse.

"That your sister?" he asked.

"Yep," I said, rolling my eyes and waiting for him to suddenly act even more interested in me. That was how it usually went the second a guy found out who my sister was. "The infamous Coco Bissett. Let me guess, you want a picture with her or something?"

He scrunched his eyes, as if he didn't know who she was. "Name sounds familiar. Don't know her, though. As I was saying…"

The whole world knew Coco Bissett. She was touted as the next Susannah Jethro, only she was a younger, more exotic, sexpot version. She had hourglass curves and legs up to her neck. She gave most Victoria's Secret models a run for their money with her long, dark waves that spilled down her voluptuous breasts and her big, baby doll eyes. Men wanted her and women wanted to be her. With an infectious laugh that put even the most nervous guest or interviewee at ease, she was easily America's next sweetheart. And that was exactly why the network was in secret talks to replace Susannah Jethro with her next year.

"You really don't know who she is?" I asked, keeping my jaw from dropping. "You don't watch the news?"

"I don't have time to watch the news. I read it," he said. "Anyway, let's get back on track here." He stepped into my space once again. "You and me. Every Friday night. Until further notice. And remember, I don't share. I should be the only one owning that exquisite pussy of yours."

"Sounds an awful lot like you want to be my boyfriend," I teased.

Wilder made a disgusted face, then his lips morphed into the smile of a man who knew he was about to get exactly what he wanted. "I'm not your boyfriend. You're not my girlfriend. And I promise never to fall in love with you."

"Likewise," I said. "I promise never to fall in love with you."

"So we have a deal?"

I shot him my best professional smile. "I'll let you know."

If several years in real estate had taught me anything, it was the art of negotiation. If the seller makes the buyer think the deal is on the verge of crumbling, it places all the power into the hands of the seller, making the buyer want it even more.

If I was going to give him my body to own, to possess, I needed him to really appreciate it. I needed him to realize property like me didn't come on the market very often, if ever.

"I'll see you Friday," he said.

"That's tomorrow."

"I know."

I strutted back to the table where Coco seemed irritated.

"Sorry about that," I said. "Ran into a friend."

"Since when do your friends look like Calvin Klein models?" Coco asked. "Sorry, I didn't mean it like that. I just meant you hadn't mentioned you had a friend who looked like that." She fanned herself. "Holy shit, he's hot."

"I may or may not have hooked up with him last night," I said coyly, pursing my lips and stifling the proud grin that wanted to plaster my face.

"Wait, what? How did you meet?" The questions continued, but I drowned them out with thoughts of him and his penetrating gaze. "Addison, you have to tell me everything. This is so unlike you. I thought you'd sworn off anything with a penis since that asshole, Kyle."

"You know that dating app everyone's using right now?" I asked her.

She furrowed her perfectly sculpted brows. "Yeah,

we just did a story on that not too long ago. It's supposed to be for dating, but most people use it to find casual sex and hook-ups."

"I was doing a little *shopping*, and I came across him," I said quietly. "It all just happened a lot faster than I thought it would."

Coco's mouth hung open in disbelief. "So you met a random stranger on a dating app and had sex with him?"

I nodded, rearranging the silverware at my place setting until the bottoms all lined up. "So unlike me, right?"

"Addison," she said, staring at me intently "Never kiss a stranger. Not in this city. You never know who you're *really* kissing."

four

WILDER

"Sorry, Aunt Laura," I said, returning to the table. "I ran into someone I know."

"Yes, I saw that," she said, studying me. "A very beautiful young woman."

I kept my face free from expression, not wanting

to give her any food for thought. Ever since my mother died, my aunt Laura had made it her business to know every detail about my personal life. She'd also made it her mission to be the one adult in my life constantly nagging me to meet a nice girl, fall in love, and settle down.

I tried changing the subject. "Where's our server? I'm starving."

A tall drink of water with straight black hair sauntered past our table, immediately bringing up an image of my ex, Nicola "Nikki" DeSoto. Nikki was a half-Dutch, half-Spanish model-slash-actress with bee stung lips and a smile that hardened my cock in mere seconds. She was also bat-shit crazy and had ruined all future relationships for me. I'd never been so sprung for a girl before I met her. I'd have moved heaven and earth, crossed oceans, and climbed mountains for her. She'd made me feel like a million bucks. I was fully convinced that I was going to marry her someday.

And then I found out she was nothing but a fucking liar. Addicted to sex and fame, she'd been sleeping her way to the top for the entirety of our relationship, all in the name of getting ahead. Never mind that she was lying in my arms at night and whispering in my ear about all the ways she loved me. She'd painted a beautiful portrait of the life we were going to live.

Together.

Forever.

She promised.

It turned out all of it was a lie. It'd been years, and I still couldn't figure out how something that felt so real could actually be nothing more than a desert mirage.

And then my mom died. The only woman who'd ever truly loved me decided her life wasn't worth living anymore and took it upon herself to end her suffering. She'd battled depression before, even moving to the sunniest parts of the country to get hefty doses of Vitamin D, as if that were all she needed. But even doped up on Zoloft and sunshine, it wasn't enough to dull the pain. All the colors in the world weren't sufficient to cover up the gray in her life. If you asked me, though, she died of a broken heart. She never really got over my dad leaving her.

In the end, she left me a multi-million dollar life insurance policy, as if that would make up for it.

"What's her name?" my aunt asked. "That girl you were talking to."

"Addison," I said. My eyes searched the room for

our server. I didn't want to talk about the piece of ass I was trying to bang as if she were some nice girl I was courting.

"What does she do for a living?"

"I don't know."

"But she's your friend. You don't know?"

"She's a *new* friend."

My aunt was relentless. Then again, she didn't have any kids and I didn't have a mother anymore. I supposed everyone needed someone like her in their lives. She made no bones about disliking the fact that I was a multi-millionaire in his twenties living in one of the most exciting cities in the world. She was quite certain that someone would swindle away my hard-earned cash or that I'd meet a gold digger who'd clean me out.

I supposed she didn't know me as well as she thought she did. If she did, she'd know that would never happen in a million years.

"What is she like?" Aunt Laura pried.

"I'm still figuring her out," I said. "Anyway, how's work?"

"Oh, same old," she said with an eye roll as she

proceeded to ramble on about her maniacal boss and the latest with her archrival, Kathy. As she went off on a tangent, I focused my gaze on the blonde beauty sitting across the room. "Wilder. Wilder, are you listening? Did you hear what I said? Your dad is getting married again. Why didn't you tell me?"

I jerked my attention back toward my aunt. "Must have slipped my mind."

"When will it end? He's becoming a joke to the family," she huffed. My dad was her younger brother, and they got along like oil and water. She kept tabs on him from afar, though, which I was certain meant she still cared about him. "Just met some woman in Kentucky. I hear they might run off to Vegas and do one of those God-awful drive-thru weddings."

"That's Vince for you," I laughed. He'd called me a couple weeks before to share the news, and I feigned excitement for him. But it was his fifth wife in fifteen years. It got old a couple wives ago. At this point, he was just making a mockery out of the whole marriage thing.

"What's her name?" my aunt asked. "Tammy Sue? Tammy Rae?"

"Tammy Lynn," I said. "As I recall."

"Where's he living now? Kentucky? How'd he end up there?"

"He says the real estate market's good there." I shrugged and grabbed a slice of warm focaccia bread from the basket between us. I'd spent my summers working in his real estate office and learning a thing or two about the business, which was how I knew exactly what to do with the millions of dollars I'd inherited from my mother when she passed. I threw it all into real estate investments.

The rest was history.

five

addison

I drummed my fingers on the marble counter of my kitchen island. Seven o'clock on Friday and not a peep from Wilder all day. I expected something. Anything but radio silence.

I'd kept my night clear on the off chance I

decided to take him up on his offer.

Oh, he was good. He knew exactly what he was doing.

I undocked myself from the island and paced my apartment. My thoughts raced, changing direction with each step. My career-oriented mind and my sexually-depraved body were at odds, and a war was being waged.

I closed my eyes as I tried to remember what he felt like inside me. How good it felt to have pure, uncomplicated sex with a man and walk away feeling satisfied. I was in independent woman. There was no shame in going out and getting laid like a man would. I just had to make sure my heart knew the difference.

"*What's one night a week?*" my body asked.

"*You know one night will turn into two and two into three, and before you know it, you'll be spending every waking hour with him. And when you're not with him, you'll wish you were. And when he decides he's done with you, it'll hurt worse than anything you've ever felt before all because you let yourself get attached,*" my brain fired back.

Fuck. Those two could go at it all night, and I needed my beauty rest. I grabbed a notebook from my meticulously organized junk drawer and a black ink pen and drew a "T" across the paper.

A pros and cons list. That ought to solve it, right? Ugh. What am I doing?

I tore the paper from the pad and crumpled it up and reached for my phone, firing off a text.

YOU WIN.

Three minutes later, he called me. "I hate texting. You forget that, lovely?"

"Sorry," I said.

"I win?"

"You win," I sighed. "But on my terms. So really, I win too."

"Your terms are?"

"No strings. No emotions. I don't even want to know your last name. I don't want to know where you're from or where you went to school. I don't want to know what your favorite color is or if you secretly love superhero movies. I don't want to know what you do for a living. Don't ask me to run out and get pancakes with you after we fuck. Don't call me at work. And don't kiss me like you love me."

"Jesus, lovely." I heard him breathe into the phone. "What the fuck did he do to you?"

"Who?"

"The last guy."

I ignored his question. It was none of his business, and we weren't supposed to get to know each other. "You're nothing more than a hard cock attached to a ridiculously attractive man, and I'm nothing more than an exquisite pussy for you to please one night a week. Nothing more. Nothing less."

His silence scared me.

"Meet me in an hour," he said at last. "Same place."

* * *

The door to the hotel suite flew open, and seconds later Wilder pulled me inside. Slamming the door, he pressed me up against it, leaning into me as his lips covered mine. His hands searched my hair, gripping hold of me by the back of my neck as he kissed me hard.

"I knew you'd come around," he growled as he

breathed me in. He stepped back and unbuttoned my coat and slipped it off my shoulders. "What are you waiting for, lovely? I want you naked and on that bed. Now. Or else."

"Or else what?" I sassed.

He scooped me up in his arms the way a groom might carry his bride and tossed me on the bed, climbing on top of me. I rolled to my stomach, pulling my hair over my shoulder. His full lips pressed into my nape as his hands slid beneath my body, gliding down to my hips where he tugged on my leggings until my thong-covered ass was exposed.

The way he worshipped my body with ease.

How natural it felt to be in bed with him.

How easy it was to hop in a cab and go to him simply because he wanted me to.

It was happening already. I could feel it. My resolve and intentions were melting away like cotton candy on my tongue.

My body demanded that my head to go on auto-pilot as Wilder had his way with me that night. It forced me to push away every thought that floated into it and just feel. I focused on the way the sheets felt as I clung to them. I concentrated on the intense fusion of pain and pleasure that seared through me as he slid himself in and out. I absorbed the sensation of his fingers raking my scalp as he gathered my hair into his hand and pulled it taut.

When it was all over, Wilder flung himself on the bed, arms spread wide as his chest heaved up and down under the pale glow of the moon. Soft beads of spring rain hit the windows, providing a relaxing soundtrack to lull us down from our euphoric heights.

And I scrambled out of the tangled covers, searching for my clothes in the dark before I had to look at him.

The light clicked on behind me. "You're leaving already?"

"I have a commitment at nine o'clock tomorrow. Some errands to run before that. Laundry…" I rambled on, giving a hundred reasons why I couldn't stay, none of which included the fact that I immensely enjoyed our time together and it scared the hell out of me.

Wilder slipped a muscled leg out of bed and raked his hand through his chocolate hair. "God, it must be exhausting being you."

"What's that supposed to mean?"

"Do you ever just loosen up? Enjoy yourself a

little?"

I tugged my pants on. "Isn't that what we just did?"

"What we did," he said with a smirk, "was the equivalent of lifting weights and then slamming an entire chocolate cake."

"I don't follow."

"You can't lose yourself in these sheets with me for an hour and then flip a switch and go right back to having a stick up your ass. Completely defeats the purpose."

"I'm not going to stay and cuddle with you."

He laughed. "Nor do I want you to. I'm not your boyfriend."

"Okay, so what's wrong with me leaving?" I shrugged. "Besides, the longer I stay, the more things I might let slip about me, and we can't have you getting to know me. I'd really hate to break your heart someday."

I threw him a wink and stepped away to grab my coat from the back of a chair. He didn't hang it up that time, but at least he'd had the decency to keep it off the hotel carpet.

Wilder shuffled across the room naked as the day he was born, like it was his preferred state, and stood before me.

"I promise you, I'm incapable of falling in love with anyone," he said, a hint of sadness flickering in his eyes. "You have nothing to worry about."

"What a relief," I said, forcing a smile and hating the fact that I wanted to know more. I wanted to know who had hurt him as bad as Kyle had hurt me.

"Let's just be who we are," he said. "You don't have to be so guarded. We're on the same page, you and me. Cut from the same cloth."

He reached for the curled ends of my silken hair, twisting a strand around his fingers before letting it fall.

"Just don't feel like you need to rush out every time I fuck you," he said. "You can stay for a minute. Take your time getting dressed. Tell me how shitty your day was until you came to see me."

I hung my head. He had a point.

"You kind of make me feel cheap," he teased. "I'm insulted."

"Don't tell me you've never been in my shoes

before," I said.

He ran his fingers across his lips as if to zip them and twisted them at the corner, locking the secret away.

"I'll never tell," he said. "Believe it or not, I'm not as big of a man whore as you think I am."

I fished around in my purse and pulled out my phone. "I better call for a cab now. I really need to get going."

"See you next Friday, lovely."

six

WILDER

She was perfect. Abso-fucking-lutely perfect. Her ripe ass. Her perky breasts. The way she didn't expect me to send her flowers after an amazing night of sex. The way she didn't turn into an emotional ball of mush after I fucked her. She didn't need to cuddle or be reassured that everything was cool with us. She didn't cry or get weird or all sentimental.

She let me dominate her naked, beautiful body, giving herself to me as we both enjoyed the hell out of ourselves.

I'd been looking for someone like her for years. No muss, no fuss. No commitment. No expectations. No reverse psychology mindfuck bullshit.

I was supposed to be able to fuck her sideways and not think about her again until the next week. I was supposed to go about my days like a man who got laid on a regular basis and didn't give a fuck about where his next lay was going to come from because he already knew.

But it didn't happen like that. I couldn't get her out of my mind. The taste of her cherry lips. The scent of her rose perfume. The way her alabaster skin felt under my palms.

I sat in my office chair Monday morning, my body aching with a restlessness that stemmed from the fact that my thoughts didn't make sense. I picked up my phone and called her.

"You're not supposed to call me when I'm working," she answered. "Did I leave something at the hotel?"

"Meet me again," I said. "Lunch. I can get another hotel room."

"Can't. I'm meeting my sister for lunch."

"Cancel."

"She'd kill me. I never cancel on her."

"Tonight," I said. "After work."

"Why are you doing this?" she asked with a hint of amusement in her tone. "You're not supposed to do this. We talked about this, remember? Once a week. One hour."

"I may have agreed to those terms and conditions, but my cock didn't sign off on it," I argued. "And I don't know if that exquisite pussy of yours did, either."

"Wilder," she shushed me. "I'm. At. Work."

"So tonight, then?"

"I have a to-do list a mile long," she countered. "I don't have time to run up to Midtown and—"

"Then I'll come to you."

"Maybe I don't want you knowing where I live."

"Then you come to me."

"You're not giving up, are you?"

"Never."

"I really do have things to do tonight." Her voice trailed as her defense faded. I could only hope she was thinking about my cock and the things it could do. "You can come over. One hour. Eight o'clock. You have to be gone by nine."

She rattled off her address and hung up.

Funny. We both lived in SoHo all this time.

* * *

That night, I knocked on a pristine, white door with APT 3B in gold lettering above the peephole.

"You're early," she said as soon as she answered.

I glanced at my watch. "Maybe ten minutes."

She stood between the door and the frame, looking me up and down. I got the feeling she didn't have a lot of people over. Shit. She probably didn't let a lot of people into her world.

"If I let you in," she said, her blue eyes softening with a thin veil of vulnerability, "just please don't break anything, okay?"

I got the feeling she wasn't talking about *things*. Not entirely, anyway. I stepped past her.

"Is this Heaven?" Everything was white or cream or some variation thereof. I was quite certain I was standing in the middle of the most immaculately unspoiled apartment in all of lower Manhattan.

"What's that supposed to mean?"

"Does anyone even live here?" There wasn't a speck of dust to be found. I slipped my shoes off. "This looks like a model unit. You can't possibly live here."

"It's not a model." She rolled her eyes and took my jacket, hanging it in a closet filled with a vast array of coats and jackets in shades of creams, grays, and blacks. "I live here."

I'd been too distracted to notice she'd been standing there in a peach silk robe the entire time, her hair piled high on top of her head. Full face of makeup, though. Of course. She couldn't let her guard down to save her life.

She shot me a sexy side smirk as I came into her space, tugging on the sash around her waist until her robe fell open.

"Oh, God," I moaned, biting my lip. Nothing underneath. "I love a girl who shows up ready to go."

I scooped her up, grabbing her lush ass as she

wrapped her thighs around my hips.

She pointed. "Down the hall." I buried my head in the inviting space of her soft cleavage as I followed her directions.

"I've been waiting for this all day," I whispered as I laid her down softly on the bed. Her knees clenched together, though she probably didn't realize she was doing it. I placed a hand on her left knee, then slid down between her thighs and parted her until she was in full bloom. As I lowered myself to taste her arousal she melted herself into the thick blankets, giving herself to me once more.

* * *

A couple hours later, I lay awake in my own bed just blocks from Addison's place. I'd left the moment we were finished, not wanting to overstay my welcome. It was maybe eleven, and I couldn't sleep. My mind kept replaying my hour with her. I'd filled the entire hour, too. I didn't want to waste a single moment with that luxurious pussy of hers.

My phone buzzed on my nightstand. A text from Addison asking if I was still awake.

I waited a moment before calling her back. "You

know I don't text."

"Sorry," she said. "I wouldn't have bothered you, but everyone else I know is asleep."

Her voice held a sort of smoky, Scarlett Johansson quality to it that instantly made my dick hard. "Why'd you assume I'd be up?"

"Am I bothering you? God. I shouldn't have called. I don't want you thinking we're friends or anything."

"Aren't we, though?"

"Can men and women ever truly be just friends?" she moaned.

"I think they made a movie about that."

"Besides, I don't like labels. I don't want to label whatever this is. It just… is what it is."

"Fair." I rolled onto my back, settling into the covers. "So, what's on your mind tonight, lovely?"

"I have this big work meeting tomorrow," she hissed. Even over the phone, I could feel her tension. "I'm really stressing out."

"What's it about?"

"I can't tell you, because I don't want you knowing what I do for a living," she said. "Basically, I'm pitching myself to this new client. But this other co-worker of mine is also pitching himself. If this client picks me, it could mean having my best year ever. Winning some awards. Growing my client list. Notoriety. Basically everything I've ever dreamed of would come true if this person chooses me."

"Who's your competition? Are they any good?"

"Yes," she said. "If I'm being honest. We're both good, though. He's just a tiny bit better. But he's such an asshole."

I laughed. "Listen, if this client of yours has an ounce of good sense about him, he'll see right through the other guy's bullshit. You just worry about yourself. You can't control what the other guy does or who the client chooses. Everything'll be fine in the end."

"Okay. You're right." She breathed in and out slowly. "I'm going to bed now. Thanks for the pep talk, coach."

"You want to meet for lunch tomorrow?" I offered. "I could take your mind off of things for a little while."

"Wilder," she laughed, "you just had me tonight. And you just had me a few days ago. This is exactly what we're not supposed to do. Once a week!"

"Come on. You know you want it again."

"I do," she admitted. "As much as I hate it to admit it. Besides, my sister wants to do lunch again today, and I already told her I would. She'll kill me if I canceled."

"All right, lovely," I sighed. "While you're eating your Cobb salad and gossiping with your dear sister, I want you to remember the way my tongue felt between your legs and the way my hair felt between your fingers as you screamed out my name."

"Goodnight, Wilder."

seven

addison

"You're glowing," Coco said as soon as I sat down. She'd beat me to the restaurant that next day. "There's something different about you."

I attempted to stifle the smile on my face, but it was no use.

"You got laid again," she whispered.

I scanned the room, wondering if I was going to

run into Wilder again like I had the last time I was out with my sister. And then I promptly scolded myself for thinking about him like that.

"Maybe." I unfolded the linen napkin from my place setting and refolded it across my lap before pushing my bread plate up two inches until it aligned with the top of my salad plate. "There. Much better."

"The, um, dating app guy," she said. "What's his name?"

"His name isn't important," I answered. "It's just a little arrangement we have."

I scanned the room one more time when a tall, dark-haired man in a three-piece suit breezed by. It wasn't him.

"You're falling for this guy," Coco said. "I can tell. It's written all over your adorable little face."

I glared at her. "I am *not* falling for him." She knew me better than anyone in the world, but I would never cop to falling for Wilder. Even if it might be true. "The sex is just really, amazingly good. That's all."

"Sure, Addison. Whatever you say." She leaned back in her seat, staring at me from the corner of her eye.

"Anyway." I had to change the subject. "Mom still hasn't told me about her new man."

"She will. You know how she is. She gets us confused so much anyway, she probably already thinks she told you."

"I'm just surprised she told you first," I said. Coco was very opinionated and wasn't afraid to give our mother an earful when she disagreed with her life choices. Though lately, Coco was so wrapped up in launching her career that she didn't seem to give a shit about our mother's personal life anymore.

"You and me both," she sighed.

* * *

"Want to split a cab?" Kyle asked as we left the office later that afternoon. I checked my watch. We had thirty minutes to get to Butter, where we were meeting Mr. Van Cleef. The idea of riding in a cab and being in such close proximity with Kyle was less appealing than plucking the hair off my head one strand at a time, but it made only sense.

"I guess," I said, walking quickly to keep a few paces ahead of him. I flew to the corner and hailed a cab, and he climbed in behind me.

"Do you know anything about this guy?" he asked.

"Nope. You?"

"Not a damn thing," Kyle said. "Hope you brought your A-game."

"You can cut the crap, Kyle."

"What are you talking about?"

"You don't have to be so 'on' all the time." I stared out the window at the passing buildings, wishing I were anywhere but in that cab with him. "You don't have to be all slimy salesman around me."

"God, you're such a bitch," he said. "No wonder we didn't work out."

"We didn't work out because you couldn't keep your dick in your pants." I briefly thought about jumping out of the cab at the next stoplight and walking the rest of the way. "Or did you forget? God, it feels like a lifetime ago."

I lied. It felt like yesterday. I fell out of love with him the day I discovered the cheating, but the sting of betrayal stayed fresh, lingering on me like a stench I couldn't wash off no matter how hard I tried.

Any relationship I ever tried to forge would be tainted from the start, thanks to the asshole sitting beside me.

The cab pulled up outside of Butter and I climbed out, heading in without waiting for Kyle.

"I'm meeting a Mr. Van Cleef," I said to the lithe young hostess dressed all in black.

She scanned her computer screen. Her eyes lit up like the Fourth of July. "Ah, yes. Wilder Van Cleef?"

Wilder? How many Wilders could there be in the city?

"Right this way," she said, ushering us to a dark corner of the restaurant where a very striking gentleman sat with his back to us.

The dark hair.

The suit.

The bold-faced Cartier watch on his wrist, which rested on the edge of the table.

It was him.

"Here you are," the hostess said with a smile before handing us menus.

I took a seat next to him. I wanted to throw up.

"Mr. Van Cleef," Kyle said, campy confidence oozing from his every pore. "I'm Kyle Maxwell of Bliss Agency, and this is my esteemed colleague and former mentee, Addison Andrews."

Mentee? I wanted to kick him in the junk right then and there, but I refrained from doing so. He was lucky.

Wilder stood up, not giving Kyle a second glance. His crystalline eyes glowed in the dim lighting of the restaurant as they locked in on me.

"Very *lovely* to meet you," he said, extending his hand to me first. He shook Kyle's hand, though only for a half second.

Kyle began to ramble on about the weather and something about the Hamptons this time of year, but Wilder appeared to tune him out.

Our table was small and intimate, more appropriate for a date than a business meeting. My knees brushed against his under the table, instantly reddening my cheeks as I recalled our night before.

"Our boss tells us you're looking for an agent who can help you find investment properties in the city," Kyle said. "Can you tell us more about what you're looking for?

Are you wanting commercial properties? High rises? Condos? Rentals?"

"A little bit of everything," Wilder said. "I like to diversify my real estate portfolio."

"Have you heard of Gotham Investments? Hillary Holdings? Pinnacle Heights Rentals?" Kyle said.

"No." Wilder scrunched his brow.

"Really? Their signs are all over the city," Kyle said. "Anyway, I've worked with all of them. I've taken companies who've started with a little bit of seed money and grown them into multi-million dollar empires."

"I've already got an empire," Wilder said. "I'm looking to expand it."

"And you're looking at the man who can do that for you," Kyle said.

Kyle lifted his briefcase to the table, whipping out pamphlets and documents and charts and graphs he'd made, all of them putting his work into numbers. He rambled on about his connections and shared anecdotal stories about sales that almost didn't happen until he slid in and saved the day.

Through conversation, they discovered they had

several mutual friends and shared connections.

"You're awfully quiet, Addison," Kyle said, a smug smile across his face as he leaned back like he'd just sealed the deal.

"Hard to get a word in with you two." The truth was I didn't feel the need to sell myself to Wilder. He knew how much it meant to me to land him as a client. I'd just told him the night before. And he couldn't possibly pick Kyle. Kyle was… *Kylo.* He was arrogant and smug, and Wilder was smart enough to see through all of it.

"So as I was saying…" Kyle continued. Wilder kept his gaze on me for a few seconds too long before turning back to Kyle.

A hand gripped my knee underneath the table on Wilder's side before inching up my inner thigh. He shot me a wink, and a fire began to ignite in my core. Words unspoken, as if we had a language all our own, forced my heart to skip two beats.

"Will you two excuse me for a second?" I had to get up, walk around, and get some fresh air. I headed to the bathroom to pat some cool water on my face, and when I emerged, I fully expected him to be waiting for me like he did the last time. But he was still back at the table with Kyle.

I counted down the minutes until our lunch was over. I just needed a few minutes alone with him, a private meeting to ensure we were on the same page with everything—personal and professional.

"I'm very sorry I have to cut this short," Wilder said as he checked his watch and stood up. "It was a pleasure meeting you both."

He shot me a wink and his lips curled into a throttled smile.

"I'll be in touch with Ms. Bliss very soon with my decision." His eyes lingered on me before he turned to walk away. The view as he left was breathtaking, and I couldn't wait to sink my fingers into his muscled glutes and feel the weight of his body pinning mine once again.

"What's with you?" Kyle sneered. "I've never seen you so quiet before. You don't want his business, or what?"

I shot him a smirk, opting not to feed into his little pissing match. He could prematurely claim victory all he wanted, but he had no idea what was about to hit him. Standing up and grabbing my purse, I slapped cash on the table and headed to the door.

A hand gripped my arm, stopping me the second I made it outside. "You can't skate by on your good looks forever."

"Do not touch me." I jerked my arm out of Kyle's grasp.

"I'm just saying, I know what men see when they look at you."

I stepped toward the curb, attempting to hail a cab and tune him out at the same time.

"They see a hot piece of ass. A one-night stand. A pair of pretty lips," he said. "And they smell it on you. The desperation. They prey on you."

Kyle must have noticed something between Wilder and me. Something set him off. Something made him feel woefully insecure about this whole competition between us.

"Like the way you preyed on me?" I said as a cab pulled up. "Not all men are like you. And thank God for that."

I climbed into the cab, trying to pull the door behind me quickly so he couldn't follow, but he stopped it mid-pull. With the door half open and a sinister leer on his face, he said, "That's where you're wrong, Addi. We're *all* the same."

I yanked the door shut, almost slamming his hand in the process, and hightailed it back to the office, wiping the tears as quickly as they fell and praying I could hold myself together long enough to get through the rest of the day.

* * *

"Addison, Brenda is calling a staff meeting," Skylar said, standing in the office doorway later that day. The office usually closed at six, and it was five-thirty. We never had impromptu meetings before closing.

I glanced at my watch. I was supposed to meet an old client for dinner that night and go over a few new listings. She was a single mom divorcée in the market for a classic six on the Upper East Side, and I had a hot listing on my hands that'd be perfect for her, though it was slightly out of her preferred price range.

"It's mandatory," Skylar said with an eye roll, as if she knew exactly what I was thinking. I supposed my perfectionist tendencies forced her to be more intuitive when it came to working for me.

We headed to the conference room. Brenda was a bundle of excited energy at the head of the long table. Her fingers twitched and flexed as she made small talk with another agent. A smile permanently fixed on her face told me she was about to announce good news.

I sat down far away from Kyle and stared out the window, wondering what Wilder was doing in that very moment.

Stop thinking about him!

"All right, everyone," Brenda said when the last agent entered the room and closed the door. "I have big news!"

"We've just landed a huge client," she said. "One of our biggest yet. His name is Wilder Van Cleef of Van Cleef Investments. He called me earlier today, shortly after meeting with Addison and Kyle, and told me he'd absolutely give us his business and that choosing his agent was an absolute no-brainer."

My lips curled into a smile, though I was the only one in the room who knew what it meant.

"He said he was blown away, and he's never met an agent of this caliber before," she continued. And then I saw her eyes travel to Kyle, who sat leaning back in his chair with his arms crossed as haughty look his sculpted face. "This contract is going to mean a lot for Bliss

Agency. And it's going to especially mean a lot for Mr. Kyle Maxwell. This very well could push him up a few spots from seventh real estate broker in all of Manhattan to maybe second or third. Who knows, maybe even first?"

"I'm shooting for first," Kyle said with a nod and a wink toward Brenda. "But I've always been a bit of an overachiever."

I refused to sit there any longer and watch their little dog and pony show while being inadvertently thrown under the bus.

And Wilder?! What the fuck?!

A storm raged inside me. My blood boiled. It may have been gray and rainy outside, but I could only see red.

"Addison? Where are you going?" Brenda called out. All eyes turned to me as I lunged for the door.

"Oh, um, I have an important meeting with a client." I glanced down at my watch. "I don't want to be late."

I wanted to add that some of us actually worked their asses off rather than bullshitting and schmoozing with the right people and fucking our way to the top.

I headed to a quaint little Italian spot in Tribeca to

meet Diane Abernathy, my sweet divorcée client. I just hoped she would cool it on the horrible ex-husband talk that night. She usually got off on a tangent and worked him into the conversation any chance she got, but I wasn't in the mood to talk about men or relationships or marriage or any of that.

I wanted to talk about condos and penthouses and apartments and townhomes. Architecture. Designers. Sale prices. Market analyses. Leases and purchase agreements. Those were the things I loved. The things that drove me. The things I understood. There was nothing complicated about any of them.

"Darling, you look ravishing!" Diane said as I greeted her at our corner table. Diane had bought and sold with me more than any other client, and now that she was divorced with a huge settlement coming her way, she was about to make her biggest purchase yet.

We kiss-kissed and I sat down, basking in the warmth of Diane's company and breathing in the tranquil cloud of her Quelques Fleurs perfume as she threw a half dozen compliments my way, mostly about my clothes and hair. It was good to forget about life for a while.

"Oh, gosh, I'm sorry," I said as my phone went off in my purse. Silencing it the moment I saw it was

Wilder calling, I turned back to her. "Now where were we?"

He called again.

Ignore.

When I finished with Diane and we went our separate ways, I checked my phone. One voicemail. One text. Wilder hated texting.

WHERE ARE YOU? I NEED TO SEE YOU. NOW. PREFERABLY NAKED.

I wanted to fire back and tell him it was none of his business, but my furious mindset would've led my fingers to type something even worse. How dare he act like nothing happened, like he could just chose Kyle over me and expect me to jump into bed with him?

Fuming, my blood boiling at a rapid pace, I fired off a text.

FUCK. OFF. WILDER.

Send.

As I walked home, I could have sworn steam blew from my red hot ears. The brisk evening air on my face helped keep the tears at bay, but it was only a matter of time before they'd creep up on me again.

I knew better.

I knew better. I knew better. I knew better.

Getting involved with Wilder had been a mistake. It was only supposed to be one night. And then nothing.

When I eventually rounded the corner to my apartment, I rode the elevator to my floor and stopped short the moment the doors parted. A very attractive man in a navy blue suit was seated on the floor in front of my door.

"What are you doing here? I thought I made it clear when I told you to fuck off." I crossed my arms as he stood up. He towered over me as he stepped into my space, making me feel small and powerless in his presence.

"I need to explain," he said. "Can I come in?"

eight

WILDER

I wanted to kiss her so bad on her heart-shaped lips the color of two red roses. I wanted to kiss away the dried tears on her cheeks.

But two things prevented that from happening:

she was livid with me and I didn't want her to know I was starting to fall for her. If she knew the way I really felt about her, she'd never talk to me again. Feelings were never part of the deal.

She consumed my every thought, proving that I was wrong all along. I was capable of feeling again. My heart wasn't permanently ruined. Banged up, scar-tissued and slightly mangled, maybe. But it was still bleeding red. The ice was thawing, and Addison was the warm sun.

She pushed past me, jamming her key into the lock and asserting her way into her apartment. I stood in the doorway, unsure if I was being invited in and watching as she threw her purse on a chair and slammed her keys on the counter.

She spun around, golden hair spilling down her face in an uncharacteristically disheveled fashion. "You going to explain, or what?"

I closed the door, stepping toward her and resisting the urge to cup her pretty face.

"The reason I picked Kyle," I said, drawing in a long, slow breath, "is because choosing you would be a huge conflict of interest."

"How so?" One perfectly arched brow raised

above one teary eye. "You and I aren't dating, Wilder. There's *nothing* between us."

"Two things you should know about me right now," I said. "I have two very distinct, very significant interests."

"Which are?"

"Real estate," I said. "And you."

She pulled away, stepping out of the tension that enveloped us, and cocked her head to the side as her brows furrowed. "Wilder…"

I pulled her back toward me, resting my hands on the dip above her hips. "I'm not saying I love you, Addison. I'm not saying I'm your boyfriend. I'm not even saying I want to date you. But this thing we're doing? Whatever you want to call it? *I love it.* I can't stop seeing you. Not yet."

She wouldn't look at me. She kept shaking her head as she stared out the living room window. Her arms hugged her sides, shielding her cool skin from the chilled April air.

"But you gave the deal to Kyle, of all people," she said. "*Kyle.*"

Kyle was a fucking jackass, of that I was certain. I'd already decided I hated the prick, and I'd spent all of one lunch with him. It was after Addison removed herself from the table temporarily that I knew exactly what I had to do.

"I see you checking her out," Kyle said to me, his voice low. "Hot piece of ass. Bat-shit crazy."

"Excuse me?" I'd asked.

"We used to date," he said. He spun his finger against the side of his head in a circular motion. "You don't want that. Trust me. She's pretty to look at. Nice lips… *if you know what I mean*. That's about all she's good for. I'd never trust her to sell a property for me."

So it was Kyle. He was the guy who had hurt Addison. Who'd made her the guarded, broken-winged baby bird I found myself irresistibly addicted to. I could've bashed his face in right then and there, but I decided to play along.

I was going to destroy him.

Professionally-speaking, anyway.

Which was precisely why I had to pick him over her. At least temporarily.

"Trust me," I said to Addison. "Everything's going to work out exactly the way it's supposed to."

"You realize I'm going to have to work extra hard now," she said. "Harder than I was working before. I have goals, Wilder. I'm not sacrificing them for *this*. I don't even know if I'll have time for *this* anymore."

My hands slid down the curves of her sides, cupping her firm ass and giving it a punishing squeeze. "Don't ever say that again."

I claimed her lips with mine before hoisting her up on the cool, marble counter top.

"I'm still angry with you," she said, ending our kiss. My lips found the indentation below her jaw and I quietly reveled in the sweet taste of her soft skin.

"You can't stay angry forever," I whispered. My right hand skimmed down her side to the opening of her skirt, then trailed along her inner thigh until it reached the silken fabric of her panties. I slid them aside and worked a finger into the inviting wetness of her folds. A faint moan passed through her lips as her head fell back, blonde hair spilling in every direction.

"Give yourself to me, lovely. You've had a long day. Just let go." I lowered myself, leveling my head between her legs and kissing the tenderness of her delicate inner thighs.

I craved her taste. Her smell. The way her fingers pulled my hair as she was just about to come. The low, sultry rasp of her voice as she begged for more. The look in her eyes when I brought her to the brink and told her not to come just yet.

The way she obeyed.

I could get lost in her for hours. An hour a week wasn't enough, and I wasn't sure it ever would be.

Addison was different. She didn't throw herself at me. She didn't pretend like most girls did. Her authenticity was addictive, and I'd never be able to resist, no matter how hard I tried.

Addison was the sun shining bright into my dark world.

And she had no fucking clue.

I was falling for her.

And she could never know.

nine

addison

My alarm blared at five in the morning, but when I leaned across the bed to silence it, my hands grazed over top of a warm body. I jerked back.

"Wilder," I whispered, pushing the hair from my face as my eyes adjusted. He squinted. "What are you still doing here?"

The light that filtered in through the curtains shown just enough for me to realize he was sleeping on top of the covers.

"You asked me to stay until you fell asleep, remember?" he said, his hair disheveled and his voice groggy. He leaned forward and rubbed his eyes.

"Are you sure? I don't remember saying that."

"You'd had a couple glasses of wine. You really don't remember?"

I shook my head. I didn't remember drinking wine, either. Then again, the day before was one of the worst days I'd had in a long time. I wouldn't have blamed yesterday-me for drinking an entire bottle of wine in an attempt to forget it.

"I'm kidding." He slid off the bed. "We were talking. I fell asleep."

I slid out of the covers, instantly realizing I was buck-naked. Pulling a sheet from the bed, I wrapped myself in it.

"Ah, you're shy in the morning," he said.

My cheeks burned hot. I was sure I'd slept off

most of my makeup, and my lashes crunched with dried mascara as I blinked. My fingers combed through the tangled knots of my hair.

The last guy to ever see me one hundred percent *au naturel* was Kyle.

I wrapped the sheet tight around my body. "Just so you know, this is something a boyfriend would do, so don't let it happen again."

I ambled toward the bathroom, starting the shower and rinsing off any remnants of the night before, hoping my confusion might swirl down the drain along with it. My life was a perfect row of dominoes I'd spent years setting up, and falling for Wilder would send them all toppling down.

My eyes closed as I faced the streaming water, letting it bead and trickle down my skin as I breathed in the warm mist. Two warm hands gripped around my waist, pulling me backwards until I was pressed against a very naked, very erect Wilder.

"What are you doing in here?" I pushed him away.

"You looked lonely in here. Thought you could use a *hand*." His right hand slid down my stomach until he reached the soft core between my thighs, slipping his fingers between my folds and massaging my clit.

The war inside me raged again, my body enjoying every second of his hands all over it and my mind reminding me that this was quickly turning into the very thing it wasn't supposed to be.

I bit my lip. "Wilder… you can't… we can't…"

He took my ear between his teeth, gently nibbling before releasing it. "This is purely physical, you and me. Just wanted to remind you."

His hand left my core and the heat from his body left my back as he lowered himself to his knees. My hands pressed against the front of the shower wall as he separated my backside and his tongue found my wetness from a completely different angle.

I'd never had an orgasm for breakfast, but I supposed there was a first time for everything.

When we were finished in the shower, we got ready side by side, sharing the marble vanity of my bathroom like we were some old married couple partaking in a morning routine.

"You smell like a sunflower," I teased him. He'd had to use all my soaps and shampoos and body lotions. "With a hint of coconut."

"I smell like you," he said with a smile that caused my heart to sink to the pit of my stomach. I wasn't sure he even knew he was smiling like that. My expression faded as I turned back toward the mirror and slicked on a smooth coat of red Chanel lipstick. "What's wrong?"

"Nothing," I lied. "Just thinking about work."

"You really can't shut it off, can you?" His head shook as he slipped on his dress pants from the night before.

"I love my job," I said, capping the tube. "I live for my job."

"Then why do you only seem like you're enjoying yourself when I'm buried in that exquisite pussy of yours?"

My cheeks warmed as I pushed him away and headed out of the bathroom. He followed, his white button down shirt in his hands.

Wilder rushed up from behind me, slipping his hands around my waist and tugging me close. "I just want to know that you're enjoying yourself even when you're not with me."

"I am," I said. At least, I thought I was. I supposed if I laid my levels of happiness side by side and compared my time with Wilder against the rest of my day, my time with Wilder would have won by a landslide. I'd never tell him that, though.

"Let's get dinner tonight," he said. "As friends."

I spun around and shot him a look. "Can't."

"Why not?"

"Because we're not friends."

His face fell slightly before a smirk took over his lips. "So if something happened to me tomorrow and you could never see me ever again, you'd be okay with that? Since we're not friends?"

"I'd miss him," I said, grazing my hand over the top of his pants where his prized cock rested. "I'd miss him so much."

I'd miss Wilder too, maybe even more than his cock, and I hated that.

He slipped his shirt on, studying my face as he fastened each button, and I stepped into a pair of red Gucci pumps.

"Guess I'll just eat dinner all by myself tonight," he said with a faux frown.

"I'm sure you have friends," I said. "Lay the guilt on me as thick as you want, but I refuse to fall for it."

My phone went off in my bag. “Sorry, I have to take this.”

He pulled his jacket and shoes on and followed me out to the hall as I took a call from a client who wanted me to show them a Brooklyn brownstone that morning. I promised him I’d do my best, but most showings needed to be arranged well in advance. As I tried to appease my client, I’d completely neglected to say goodbye to Wilder. I was already outside, heading up the street to the office, and he was nowhere to be seen.

By the time I slid into my desk and placed a call to the listing agent on the brownstone, my phone rang again, forcing my heart to skip a beat. I knew who it was, and I knew he wasn’t going to drop the dinner thing.

“You’re just not giving up on this, are you?” I said as I answered.

“Hello? Addison? Addison, is that you?” It was my mother, Tammy Lynn.

“Oh, sorry, Mom, thought you were someone else,” I said.

“Oh, that’s fine, sweetheart,” she said in her full, Kentucky drawl. “The reason I’m callin’ you is because I have a bit of news to share.”

"I heard," I said. I couldn't even fake excitement for her. At this point, she was just making a fool of herself by getting married more often than she replaced her vehicles.

"Heard what?" She loved to play dumb.

"That you're engaged to some guy," I said. Thank God she couldn't see my massive eye roll.

"He's not just any guy, Addison," she said. "He's the greatest guy I've ever met in my entire life. I can't wait for you to meet him and his son."

"One big, happy family," I said as I responded to an email.

"We're going to come to the city in a couple weeks," she said. "We'd like for the five of us to spend a little time together, and then he's going to spend some time with his son, and I'll spend some time with you and Dakota."

Mom still refused to call Dakota "Coco," claiming she'd be damned if she called her anything other than her Christian name.

"Okay, so two weeks from tomorrow, we'll be arriving in the Big Apple," she twanged. "Can't wait to see you, sugar. I'm gonna let you go now. My man is taking me out for breakfast."

"Don't you have to work?"

She giggled. "He's also my boss."

I lowered my head, faux face-palming. No one had ever accused Tammy Lynn Andrews of having a lick of common sense when it came to her choices in men.

ten

WILDER

"I knew you'd come around," I said as the host escorted Addison to the table. The fresh coat of lipstick and the faint breeze of flowers that floated off her body told me she'd freshened up before coming.

It'd taken most of the afternoon and a few back and forth phone calls, but I'd eventually convinced her to meet me for dinner.

"Kind of nice to relinquish control outside of the bedroom, isn't it?" I whispered as I leaned across the table.

When I looked into her pretty blue eyes, I saw a tightly wound woman with scars as deep as the ocean. I fully intended to peel back her layers one by one and get to the heart of who she really was.

I wanted to know what made her tick. And it wasn't because she was pretty or a good lay. Meeting Addison was like cracking open an oyster and finding an enormous pearl. For the vast majority of my twenties, the oysters I'd cracked had been empty.

Maybe I didn't deserve her, and I sure as hell didn't know what to do with her, but I'd found her. What was that saying? Finders, keepers?

"This looks like a date, Wilder." Her lips turned down at the corners as she feigned disappointment. I only knew she was faking it because the flickering candle between us threw soft shadows on her face, illuminating the fact that her eyes were all lit up.

"There's something I've been meaning to ask you." I cleared my throat.

Her eyes widened. "Um, okay?"

"Will you… will you be…" I purposely drug it out to torture her. "My friend?"

She buried her face in her hands, shaking her head. And when she lifted her gaze to meet mine, she was grinning. "You scared me."

"Can we be friends?" I was completely serious. "I want to call you my friend."

"You're falling for me." She cocked her head to the side. "I knew this would happen."

"I'm not falling for you," I lied.

"I'm in love with my job, Wilder," she said, speaking about it as if it were a living, breathing entity and I was just a torrid affair.

The server approached, cutting our conversation off and taking our orders. We spent the rest of the dinner making small talk, with Addison making concerted efforts to avoid speaking about anything remotely personal, and we headed outside the moment I'd paid the check.

"Thanks for dinner… *friend*." She poked her finger into my chest. Her pretty lips opened wide into a yawn. "You wore me out last night. I need to go home and go to bed."

"It's only eight o'clock," I objected. "The night's young… *friend.*"

I reached for her arm, but she yanked it away before I had a chance to pull her in. "Not tonight."

She stepped toward the curb as a Yellow Cab approached, flagging her arm high in the air. The cab came to a screeching halt and she tugged the door open, turning to me to wave goodbye.

Something came over me in that moment, and I found myself climbing into the cab alongside her.

"What are you doing?" she asked with a bewildered look in her eyes.

I gave my address to the cabbie and pulled Addison onto my lap, my hands finding her mouth in the dark of the backseat as city lights played across the side of her face like a movie scene. Pulling her face to mine, I kissed her like I meant it.

"I'm taking you home with me tonight."

* * *

No woman I'd been involved with in the last few years had set foot in my apartment. Not since Nikki. My space was sacred. And bringing girls home usually gave them the wrong impression, anyway.

"Nice," she said as we rode the elevator to my penthouse. I'd purchased it after I made my first ten million, one year after my mom passed. "This is beautiful." She kicked off her candy-apple-colored heels and toed across the room to the slider that went to the balcony. "I had no idea we were neighbors, either. When were you going to tell me?"

"You didn't want to know anything about me."

Sometimes it felt wrong living there, as if it were paid for by my mother's death in some fucked up, roundabout way. But my aunt reminded me that it was what my mother would have wanted. She would've wanted me to live comfortably with the world at my fingertips, the way she never could.

I came up behind Addison, slipping my hands around her waist and bringing them up to her ripe breasts. My lips found the curve between her jaw and her neck as she melted into me.

"I don't know if I have the energy." Her words were a faint whisper. She turned to face me, halting my opportunity to devour her inch by inch. "Please. Stop doing do this."

"Stop doing what? I'm doing a lot of things right now, lovely. You're going to have to be more specific."

"Stop making me fall for you."

Frozen by her plea, I obliged, letting my hands fall away from her soft skin.

"I told you you could control my body." Her words were broken and jagged, her crestfallen face laced with regret. "But I never said you could control my heart. I didn't want to get to know you. I didn't want to let you in. I didn't want to give two shits about anything other than…"

Her words trailed off, her eyes landing on the acid stained concrete floor.

"I should go." She pushed past me, stepping into her shoes and getting back on the elevator.

With my hands in my pocket and words caught in my throat, I watched her go.

eleven

addison

"Coco, can I come over?" I asked as I stood outside Wilder's apartment building. Glancing over my shoulder every two seconds, I just prayed he didn't follow me outside. Then again, he didn't talk me out of leaving. He didn't stop the elevator. He let me go.

"Addison, it's late," she said. "Aren't you usually in bed by now?"

"Aren't you?" I asked. She usually got up around three to get ready for work.

"Come on over," she said.

* * *

"Hi, Harrison," I said as I stepped into their loft. He glanced up from his weathered leather chair, his feet kicked up on the ottoman as he did a New York Times crossword.

"Pleasure to see you, Addison." His words were dry, and I watched as he glanced up at the clock above the mantle. I knew it was well past a proper visiting hour, but I needed my sister. Harrison always had a stick up his ass, anyway. I'd learned over the years to let him roll off my back. Most of the time, I'd razz him back and call him out when he was being a giant asshole, and we'd laugh and be fine. But I wasn't in the mood that night.

The fireplace glowed, bringing a warmth to their home that I'd come to love over the years. I'd found them their apartment years ago when they were just newlyweds. Before she'd landed the spot on the morning news show. Before they'd thrown in the towel on what seemed to be a perfect union.

Coco's fiercely guarded nature rivaled mine, though, and she never did tell me exactly why she'd divorced him. She never did tell me exactly why they were still living together two years later, either.

Coco left Harrison, at least on paper, around the same time Kyle and I had crumbled to the ground. Too many times she'd set her own personal issues aside so she could deal with mine. She was amazing like that. Coco wasn't just my big sister, she was my best friend. My protector. My person.

"Come on in," she said. "Ignore him."

"Not getting along today?" I whispered.

She rolled her eyes. "He's got a giant stick lodged up his ass right now."

"The one that's been there for years?"

"Yep. The one passed down from generation after generation of Bissetts before him." Coco lead us down the hall to the master suite, the one she inhabited all by herself. Somehow she'd convinced Harrison to take up residence in the guest suite.

I perched on the foot of her bed, the same place

I'd spent curled up in an inconsolable ball the night I found out about Kyle and all of his indiscretions. The same place I laid when I swore off men and love and romance and anything else that could make me feel.

I told her I was going to be independent and self-sufficient to a fault. I'd never let another man control my heart again. I'd never rely on another man to boost me up, either, professionally or socially. I could do it all on my own. My heart wrapped itself in barbed wire that night.

"So, what's going on?" Coco asked. She looked completely different without her camera-ready face on, though she was still gorgeous. We shared the same almond-shaped eyes and heart-shaped, swollen lips. With our high cheekbones and long necks, we looked like two aristocratic sisters born in the wrong century.

Who'd have thought we were a couple of dirt-poor Kentucky girls who'd flown from the only nest we'd known in search of something better for ourselves?

Tears stung my eyes. My attempts to blink them away were useless.

"Uh-oh." Coco scooted closer to me, rubbing her hand against my back. "What'd the bastard do to you?"

A knock at her door pulled her away from me for

a second.

"What do you want?" she said as she pulled the door open. Harrison's muffled voice on the other side seemed to be asking her a question. Or telling her to do something. Probably the latter. "No, I told you. No. I'm not. You'll have to find someone else to do that interview."

Harrison said something else that I couldn't make out.

"Never in a million, billion years. I'm not doing that interview," Coco said, stomping her foot into the carpet. "I'm with my sister. I don't know why you're picking right now to discuss this."

She slammed the door, looking flustered and red-faced as she returned to her spot next to me.

"I'll never understand why you two still live together," I sighed, almost grateful to not be talking about my issue.

"It just works." She shrugged. "And you know why? It's because I don't care. Once you care, you're fucked. But if you don't care, you find you can really put up with a lot. If Harrison walked out tomorrow and found his own place, I'd be thrilled. It's because I don't care."

I didn't believe it for one second, but I didn't have the energy to argue with her on that fact. We'd gone rounds on it before, and I'd lost every time. Coco was quick on her feet whenever she had to defend her life choices.

"What if you wanted to date someone new?" I asked. "You can't bring him to the house you share with your ex-husband."

She pursed her lips, looking at me funny. "You know I don't have time to date."

It was true. When she wasn't anchoring the weekend news, she was being flown around the world to anchor the Olympics or various royal weddings.

"Anyway, enough about me. What's going on with you? You never come over this late."

"I had dinner with Wilder today," I said.

"Oh, so he does have a name."

"We were supposed to hook up one time, Coco. One time. I let him talk me into another. And another. And then he stayed the night. And then we had dinner." My shoulders fell, as if the weight of the issue was too heavy for them to bear a second longer. "He invited me over tonight."

"Sounds like he might actually be a nice guy."

"That's the problem. I'm starting to like him. I didn't want it to get this far. I've completely fucked myself over."

"How so?"

"If I walk away from him," I said, "I'm going to miss him like crazy. I'll always wonder what might have been. And if I stay, try to make this work with him, whatever it is, I know myself—I can't juggle my career and a relationship with someone like him. I already have too much on my plate. And I don't want to get hurt again—"

"Addison, stop." Coco placed her hand on mine. "Slow down. You're getting all worked up over this. You need to let go of this notion that you can control everything."

I huffed. Coco Bissett was telling the world's biggest control freak she couldn't control a damn thing anymore.

"You can't control the way you feel about this guy," she said. "You can't force yourself not to like him. And you can't control whether or not you get hurt again."

"You're right." I sucked in a deep breath. Coco's room smelled like lavender and vanilla, a far cry from the second-hand smoke scented trailer bedroom we'd once shared. I ran my hand over the soft fabric of her duvet, the one we'd picked out together when I'd helped her with her wedding registry at Neiman Marcus years ago. I bet when we were picking it out, she never thought she'd be sleeping on it alone just a few short years later. "Do you ever regret marrying Harrison?"

"Never." She didn't miss a beat. "I loved him, Addison. We had some amazing years together. We might fight like cats and dogs, but I wouldn't trade our history for the world."

I brought my fingers across my lips, remembering the way Wilder felt when he'd kissed me in the cab. He liked me. He really liked me. All I ever did was be myself around him, and he liked me anyway.

"So if you're asking if I think you should be with this guy," Coco said, "my answer is yes. If you like him, be with him. Don't worry about everything else. It'll all fall into place."

"I need time to think about all this." I tucked a wisp of hair behind my right ear. "This just happened so fast."

"All right. Give yourself a deadline. Give yourself

until the end of the week to decide what you want to do."

An intense fatigue washed over my body from head to toe, though I suspected some of it was emotional and not physical. "I should get going. It's late."

"You feel better?" Coco asked. "Get everything off your chest like you wanted?"

We stood and I wrapped my arms around my sister, breathing in her fabric softener and Jo Malone fragrance before she walked me to the door.

"Call me if you need anything, okay?" she said as she watched me leave. And I could've sworn I heard her whisper, "*Don't be scared, little sister.*"

Though it might have been a childhood memory playing in my ear. She'd always been my voice of reason, and the one person I turned to when I didn't know where else to turn. Her answer for everything was always a simple, "Don't be scared, little sister."

* * *

I'd left Wilder a voicemail that night, telling him I needed some space. I didn't elaborate or go on. I didn't give him false hope or twist the knife I'd just stabbed him with. I simply told him I needed space.

And space he gave me.

I searched for him everywhere I went, wondering if I'd run into him as I dined with clients or as I rounded the street corner by my apartment. I searched for him as I hosted open houses, wondering if he'd stop in. I'd glance into Kyle's office when I passed, wondering if they happened to be meeting. But worst of all, my hands searched for him in the early morning hours, remembering that morning he'd stayed with me all night.

I lost myself in my work. Closings. Offers. Showings. Tours. Leads. Meetings. Market analyses. Listings. Rental and purchase agreements. If I stayed busy enough, I was fully convinced I'd forget about him for a bit. I needed my palette cleansed. Wilder was looping through my brain like an earworm, and I'd already memorized his taste, his touch, the way he felt inside me. The way his voice reverberated low and against my eardrum, sending my body into hysteria.

I never ran into him. And I never stopped thinking about him. Especially at the end of the day, when I had no work to do. When the T.V. was off and the phone was quiet. When the pitch black of my room swallowed me whole and the cool sheets wrapped around my body made me long for someone warm to curl up with.

Those were the moments Wilder invaded my thoughts with a vengeance.

* * *

"You're unusually late today." The second I entered the office the next morning I found Brenda Bliss standing at Skylar's desk. I was only twenty-seven minutes late, if she wanted to get technical.

Ever since I started working for her, I'd arrived at a quarter 'til eight on the dot each weekday. My routine was always the same. Check in at work. Contact leads from the night before and follow up with clients. Look for any new listings that may have popped up overnight. Check my schedule and spend the rest of the day meeting clients and buzzing around the city showing properties. I'd check back in at the end of the day unless I had a client dinner, then I'd go home. Rinse. Repeat. Brenda kept a close watch on all of us, memorizing our schedules because she had nothing better to do in that giant office of hers.

"I had a showing this morning," I lied. The truth was that I'd caught a wild hair on my walk to work that morning. Halfway up my street, I decided to take a detour and head to Wilder's block. I stood in his lobby and buzzed his penthouse, only he didn't answer. I called him once, but he didn't answer his phone, either.

After leaving his building, I took a detour to a coffee shop and got the biggest mocha cappuccino on the menu and tacked on a giant banana chocolate chip muffin. I stopped on a park bench and enjoyed the hell out of my breakfast.

I just wanted to prove to myself that I didn't need my routines to be okay. That no matter what happened with Wilder, I was going to be fine. Giving up control of my routine, the one thing that made me feel so safe and powerful, was the most liberating thing I'd ever done.

"I need to see you in my office," she said, nodding toward her open door. "Now."

My heart pounded, rising into my throat as I followed her. The muffin from earlier suddenly felt heavy as it sloshed around in my stomach like thick sludge. Private meetings with Brenda always gave me mini panic attacks.

"Have a seat, Addison," she said, her voice quiet as she shut the door behind us. She took a seat in her ultra-luxe leather chair and scooted in. "I wanted to speak with you regarding our newest client, Mr. Van Cleef."

My throat tightened as I felt the color drain from my face.

"This comes as a complete surprise to me," she said, "but Mr. Van Cleef is entirely disappointed with Kyle."

I clenched my lips together, fighting off the smile that so badly wanted to emerge. It took everything I had not to tell her, "I told you so."

"He says he wants the blonde," Brenda said with a shrug. "He wants you. Matter of fact, he's waiting for you right now. In your office."

I left Brenda's office and headed to mine, where my stomach did somersaults the moment my eyes landed on the back of his chocolate brown head of hair.

"Good morning, Mr. Van Cleef," I said in my most professional tone. He turned around slowly, his face lighting up the second our eyes met. I closed the door behind me and headed to my chair. "I'm sorry to hear Mr. Maxwell didn't work out for you."

"Yes," he said. "I made sure to tell Brenda how deeply disappointed I was in working with Mr. Maxwell, and how unprofessional he has been on the job."

I swallowed, almost certain my gulp was quite audible. Did he know about Kyle and me?

"I mentioned to her how having a team member

like Mr. Maxwell was basically committing real estate agency suicide," he continued. "It could be very bad for business to have an agent with such poor ethics on your team. She seemed to agree."

"Did you tell her to fire him?" I squinted at him from across my desk.

"In not so many words."

"But why?"

"I have my reasons," he said. "Besides, I'd much rather work with you, and now that we're not fooling around, I'd like to hire you on."

"I didn't know we were officially no longer fooling around." I crossed my arms.

"You made your intentions very clear that night I brought you home with me."

"Oh, really?"

"When you ran out of my penthouse and then told me to give you space after I'd just declared my feelings for you, I assumed that meant you wanted space from both of us." His eyes landed on his bulge of his cock for just a moment. "We're sort of a package deal."

Wilder stood up, walking around the desk and

coming to my side. He pulled me up and wrapped me in a strong embrace.

"I can't do the no-strings thing anymore," he said. "Not with you. Any other girl, sure. Not you."

I swallowed the lump in my throat, but it returned in an instant.

"I can't keep fucking you and looking into those empty eyes," he said. His hand cupped my chin, lifting my mouth to his yet holding himself just far enough away to prevent our lips from actually meeting.

"My eyes may have been empty," I admitted, my tone meek, "but my heart never was. You just couldn't see it."

And with those words, I'd erased the line I'd drawn in the sand the night I met him; the line that had been crossed over and over again.

"So it's settled," he said. "You'll be my agent *and* my girlfriend."

twelve

WILDER

"I ordered your usual," my aunt said as she dipped a slice of bread into a saucer of olive oil. "I'm sorry, Wilder. I was starving. And you're late." She rolled her eyes, though I knew she couldn't stay mad at me for long.

"Aunt Laura," I said as I met her for our weekly

dinner. I kissed her cheek and sat down across from her, still wearing the smile Addison had given me earlier that day.

"Well, you're awfully chipper tonight," she said. She leaned back in her seat, giving me a once over as she chewed. "What's all this about?"

"Just had a pretty amazing day," I said. I turned the tables on her. "How about you?"

"Oh, same old." She rolled her eyes as she proceeded to vent again about her work arch nemesis, Kathy. "You know, I talked to Vince today."

She always had to bring up my dad, though I supposed he was the common thread between us.

"He said he's coming to the city with his new fiancée," she said, one eyebrow raised. "Were you aware he was coming to town?"

"Yeah, he called me the other day and said something about it," I said. "I wasn't really listening."

It was the night Addison ran out of my apartment. My mind was elsewhere, so I only picked up bits and pieces of what he was saying. He always tended to call late at night, too, neglecting to consider the time difference between us.

"He said something about doing dinner with her and her two daughters," I said. "That's about all I picked up from the conversation. I was a little preoccupied when he called."

"I mean, how well can he really know this woman?" Aunt Laura scoffed. She'd been single most of her life after a failed marriage in her early twenties. Brash and opinionated, she was more than most men could handle, and yet she still believed she just hadn't met the right one yet. For all her hard edges and straight lines, she really was a hopeless romantic. "It can't possibly be true love."

I shrugged. "Who are we to say whether or not the man's in love, right? To each their own."

"Well, given your father's track record…"

"Maybe he's finally met the One? We'll have to see what she's like. He does sound happy, I'll say that."

She laughed. "Good for Vince."

"What about you? You go on any dates lately?"

"One." She slipped a finger coyly into the corner of her mouth. "His name is Steven Goldberg. He's my accountant."

"Aunt Laura…" I said in jest, as if she'd revealed a scandalous secret. "Look at you, mixing business and pleasure. You rebel."

"Oh, stop." She giggled like a schoolgirl, her hardened expression fading, if only temporarily. "It was just one date. But I will tell you, he's a phenomenal kisser." Her fingers flew up as she placed air quotes around the word "kisser."

I shielded my eyes, hanging my face. I couldn't look at her. "I didn't ask for details."

"Oh, come on, at least one of us is getting some," she whispered.

I lifted my eyes and focused on the bread basket, unable to meet hers. I wanted to leave. The conversation took a sharp detour to the bad part of town, and I couldn't get out of there fast enough.

"Wait a minute," she said. "What happened to that pretty girl you saw at the restaurant a few weeks ago? Your friend? What was her name?"

"Addison," I said.

"You still talk to her?"

"I do."

"Tell me about her." Aunt Laura twisted her wine glass in her fingers as her attention honed in on me. "I want to know everything. She's the reason you're glowing right now, I just know it. I haven't seen you light up like this in years."

"I'm glowing?" I laughed.

"You're glowing like a damn pregnant lady," she said. "Now spill it. Tell me everything. Where is she from, what is she like? Does she have any family? Where does she work?"

"She works in real estate," I said.

"Ah, so she's right up your alley."

"She's driven. Independent. Way too stubborn," I said, fondly recalling her. "Beautiful inside and out."

And then it hit me. I still barely knew her. The only thing I knew for sure was that I wanted to know everything about her.

Thoughts of Addison buzzed through me like a live wire, as my aunt took her sweet time finishing her dinner. The second I paid the check, I bolted out of there. I had to get to her.

thirteen

addison

Two weeks later…

Morning sex was my favorite. No, maybe it was shower sex. Maybe it was a tie. I wasn't sure. Days and weeks blended together into one giant mess of sex and love-drunk, late night conversations and sleep overs.

I rolled over in bed, curling up into my brand

new, bona fide boyfriend's arms and sliding a free hand down his boxers until it reached his rock solid morning wood. I slid down the length of his muscled torso until my lips found his shaft.

Wilder moaned as he stirred awake. Never one to waste an erection, especially when they were attached to the world's hottest man, I took the tip of his cock in my mouth.

"Oh, God, that feels amazing…" he moaned as his hands reached the top of my head, tangling his fingers into my messy bedhead.

Who was this girl? This girl who lived for the moment all of a sudden. Who pushed her cares away and focused all her attention on the man with the golden touch. The man who held more power over her than she could ever possibly hold over her own self.

I was changing. I hardly recognized myself. And I loved the new me.

Coco had called me Addison 2.0 at lunch the day before, saying whatever I was doing was working. I failed to tell her I was falling in love. That was my secret. She said I looked as if I'd bottled up a billion stars and bathed in them before slathering them all over myself like Crème de la Mer.

I hadn't made my bed in days. Wilder had been sleeping over every night for the past two weeks. And I'd scaled back on my overly zealous work schedule in an attempt to make time for him. I'd scaled back on a lot of things. In the two weeks since I'd last ran on my treadmill, I'd gained a good five pounds. When you removed running from your routine and replaced it with decadent dinners at New York's finest restaurants, that sort of thing was bound to happen. But Wilder said he loved every inch of me anyway. He swore he couldn't even tell, and I believed him.

Everything was working out perfectly. Almost too perfectly. I refused to believe that we were meant to be anything other than lovers in love.

I finished worshipping Wilder's delectable cock and wiped the corner of my mouth before climbing up his body. We slept naked every night, keeping warm by the mixed heat of our bodies under the covers. With my cheek against his bare chest, Wilder traced his fingers along the side of my jaw.

"I'd kiss you right now, but…" he whispered.

"It's okay." I gripped him tighter, tucking my

hand under his side. "I just want to lay here for a bit."

He let me linger for a while before gently nudging me off him. "I'm going to hop in the shower."

I watched his fine ass as he strutted out of my room. He was mine. Wilder Van Cleef was mine.

And every cell in my twenty-five-year-old body was his.

"Oh, forgot to tell you," he said as he popped his head back in the doorway. "Can't do dinner tonight. My dad's in town. I'm supposed to go meet his new wife, or some shit like that." He sauntered back toward the bed, placing a kiss on my forehead. "Believe me, I'd rather be spending the evening with you."

* * *

"Why are you acting so weird?" Coco asked as we shared a cab to dinner that night. We were headed to meet our new stepfather-to-be and his son, who coincidentally also lived in the city.

I hadn't said anything to Wilder. When he mentioned he was meeting his father's new family the same night I was supposed to meet my mother's new fiancé, a sickness had settled in the pit of my stomach.

I thought maybe if I didn't think about the fact that our relationship seemed to be entwined in coincidence, it wouldn't be true. Stranger things had happened, of that I was sure. We couldn't possibly be the children of two people who were planning to marry.

Though we were still in the getting-to-know you phase, we'd talked about our parents and found humor in the fact that they were both love addicts, but we'd never talked details beyond that. I knew his dad's name was Vince, but that was it.

"Hey, what's Mom's fiancé's name?" I asked Coco.

She scrunched her nose. "It starts with a V. Vance, maybe? No. Vince. I think it's Vince. Pretty sure. Why?"

The words refused to come out. If I didn't say it out loud, it couldn't possibly be true. I waved her off, thanking the stars when a text message on her phone stole her attention.

The cab dropped us off in front of a quaint little French bistro in the East Village. From the sidewalk, we saw Mom and her new guy sitting at a table by the window. His thick head of chocolate brown hair was flecked with gray at the temples, and though his paunch gave away his age, his profile was strikingly similar to Wilder's.

This isn't happening. This isn't happening. This isn't happening.

My legs threatened to give out from underneath me with each step we took toward the restaurant. I wanted to turn and run. I wanted to pretend this was all a bad dream. An alternate reality. A glitch in the matrix. That I wasn't about to find out that the man I was falling in love with wasn't going to be off-limits in every sense of the word.

"Girls!" my mom chirped the moment she saw us. She popped up out of her seat, her blonde hair hanging in loose curls around her face. She looked older since the last time I saw her. I focused on the lines stacked across her forehead as I avoided looking Vince's way. "Vince, this is my oldest daughter, Dakota."

Vince stood up and shook Coco's hand. She smiled like the classy woman she'd become over the years and took a seat.

"And this is my baby, Addison," my mom gushed. She wrapped her arm around my side and pulled me in.

"Everybody says we look just alike."

I stared at the empty seat next to Vince as my mom rambled on about our identical features. I supposed we did look similar. We were flesh and blood, after all. But Tammy Lynn's face had been weathered and leathered over the years. She'd lived a hard life. A beauty queen who peaked in high school, she never quite noticed when her looks gradually faded over the years. The only time her age seemed to blur was when her eyes lit up and her full lips twisted into a smile.

Men seemed to gravitate toward her infectious laugh, big boobs, and her ability to morph into whatever the hell kind of girlfriend they wanted her to be. After they got tired of her tofu personality, they usually moved on to something else. It happened every time.

"Hi, Addison." Vince extended his right hand, and I returned the gesture, forcing myself to look him in the eyes.

Those eyes.

Those aquamarine eyes that matched the very ones I lost myself in on a nightly basis. Two tropical lagoons that made the rest of the world fade away, if only for an hour or two.

"Sorry I'm late," a man's voice startled me back into the moment. But it wasn't just any man's voice.

"Wilder, my boy!" Vince said, wrapping his son in a big bear hug. He looked at Wilder like he wanted to ruffle his fingers through his hair. "Dakota, Addison, this is my son, Wilder."

Wilder's face fell as our eyes met. He offered a cordial smile to my mother as he shook her hand, and we all found our seats as soon as the server brought by a tray of water.

"So," my mother said, grinning wide and clasping her hands together as she stared into Vince's eyes. Judging by the way she was acting, it may as well have been Christmas morning. All she ever wanted was a nuclear family, like the ones she grew up watching on T.V. in the sixties and seventies. A modern-day *Brady Bunch* or *Leave it to Beaver*. "How about this. Girls, you always said you wished you had a brother growing up. How old are you, Wilder?"

"Twenty-seven," Vince answered for him. "He'll be twenty-eight next month. On the first of May."

"Oh, so you're Dakota's age," my mom said with a smile as she nudged Dakota. "Dakota, how's work going these days? I watch you on T.V. every single morning. My goodness, my DVR queue is just full of all the shows I've saved of yours."

Coco and I exchanged looks. There was Tammy Lynn pretending to be Mother of the Year again. She never gave two shits about us growing up. I could recall countless track meets where I'd look up into the bleachers to find that Coco was the only person cheering me on, and the ache in my stomach from going to bed hungry so many nights never fully went away, no matter how many years had passed.

"Mom couldn't make it," or "Mom's not feeling well" was how Coco would cover for her, though it was always for my benefit. Lies or no lies, I knew the truth. She was usually sleeping off a hangover or on a three-day bender with her newest boy toy.

I took a good look at my mother. In her khakis and a merino wool twin set the color of sea mist, she looked like she belonged at a country club. Never mind the pearl necklace dangling over her sun-freckled décolletage. What did Vince see in her? In his golf polo and gray slacks, he was a far cry from all of the men I'd ever seen her with.

Tofu. That was it. He could mold her and flavor her however he saw fit. He probably didn't even realize he was doing it. Tammy Lynn was pretty good about picking up on what men wanted and almost shape-shifting herself to fit their mold.

She seemed happy, though.

"Addison," Wilder whispered from across the table, reminding me of the real issue at hand. The one I refused to acknowledge until I could get my thoughts straight.

If I looked at him, I knew I'd cry. I grabbed the drink menu and searched long and hard for the strongest drink I could find.

"So how'd you two meet?" Coco asked as she sipped her water.

"I answered an ad for a job in the paper working at a real estate agency," Mom said, the lilt in her voice suggesting she was recalling one of the greatest moments of her life. "Vince happened to own the agency."

Vince's lips danced into a smile, as if he recognized the impropriety of the origins of their relationship. "I couldn't resist your mother, Dakota. I mean, look at her. She's beautiful and kind. Everything I could want in a woman. And the way she spoke about her daughters told me she was a wonderful mother, too. A real catch."

Wilder cleared his throat and kicked me under the table. My gaze was still transfixed on the miniature vase in the center containing a single white rose the color of a wedding day, sitting pretty and innocent amidst five complicated souls.

"So, Wilder, what is it that you do again?" My mom's voice held a softer, more matronly quality in it than it ever did when we were kids. "Vince says you followed in his footsteps?"

"Not quite," Wilder said. He spoke to my mom, but his eyes were on me. I could feel the weight of his stare, as if he were silently pleading for me to look at him. "I deal mostly with investments. Flipping properties. Finding buildings to renovate and rent out. I got my first taste of the business as a child, though, working in my dad's office."

"Smart boy, this one." Vince beamed as he rubbed Wilder's back. I couldn't watch.

"My Addison works in real estate!" my mom said. "Do you two know each other?"

I shook my head fervently before Wilder had a chance to say anything. "We don't."

"Have we all had a chance to look at our menus?" the server asked, appearing out of nowhere.

My stomach churned. Anything I were to attempt to eat was going to come right back up.

"I can order something for you, if you'd like," Wilder offered. "I bet you'd like the duck a l'orange."

We'd just shared a duck dinner a week ago. Before we knew we were going to be stepsiblings. When our biggest concern was when and where our next hot and heavy fuck session was going to take place.

"No, thank you." I closed my menu.

"Addison, don't be rude," my mom said with an incredulous laugh. Her elbow landed gently against my rib cage. "Your new brother is trying to be cordial to you."

My new brother? Were we five?

Vince and mom stared at each other with a secret knowing look in their sparkling eyes. I had to admit, I'd never seen her so happy before, and Vince was a thousand steps up from her usual type.

"We have a teeny tiny little confession to make," my mom said, her eyes shifting from Vince's to the sparkling ring on her finger. I looked a little closer. There was an extra band next to her engagement ring.

Vince nodded, as if quietly giving her permission to go ahead and tell us their news.

"Vince and I got married two weeks ago!" Her mouth twisted into the kind of smile I'd only seen once before, in the picture on her dresser from when she was crowned homecoming queen in high school. Tammy Lynn was acting as if she'd just won the fucking lottery. "We just couldn't wait."

She reached across the table, placing her hand over his.

"I just love this woman so much," Vince said. For a grown man, his fidgeting could rival a lovesick teenager's. "I had to nail her down before she got away."

Trust me, she's not going anywhere. She's like a bloodsucking leech. You'll have to peel her off you.

"Oh, God," I said, covering my mouth with my hands as the pit of my stomach twisted violently. Whatever remained in my stomach from lunchtime was moving upwards. I had to stand up. I had to walk. My lungs gasped for air.

I've been fucking my stepbrother for the last two weeks.

"Excuse me." I scooted away from the table and made a beeline for the front door, and from the corner of my eye, I saw Coco running after me and I thought I heard my mom say something about how I always got upset when she had a new "friend" in her life.

"What's going on?" Coco asked the second we burst through the doors. My lungs gasped for fresh air. "You act like you're surprised or something. This is totally Mom."

I peered over her shoulder, glancing back toward the restaurant where Mom, Vince, and Wilder seemed to be immersed in conversation; only Wilder's piercing stare was honed in on me.

"Wilder…" I began to say. The words got stuck in my throat. If I said them, that would mean it was all real. I loved a man I couldn't be with. "Wilder is…"

"Wait a minute." Coco placed her hand up and stopped me. "That's… that's the guy. The Calvin Klein model. The guy you met… that you've been… the one you…"

Coco stepped back, clutching at the diamond pendant dangling around her delicate neck. Horror washed over her face.

"You can't," she said. "You have to end it now."

"I know," I whined, staring back and allowing our eyes to lock for a brief moment.

"He's our *stepbrother* now," Coco said, crossing her arms. "It has to end. We have reputations in this city, Addison. Page Six would eat us alive with that sort of gossip! Our careers would be over."

She began pacing frantically. Coco's star was rising, and her career had been on an upward trajectory over the last few years. She had major dreams. Dreams I'd promised to do whatever it took to support, since I knew she'd do the same for me.

"If anyone finds out," Coco said, her voice breaking, "I'll be a laughingstock. You too. Especially you."

"I know, Coco." I hung my head.

"Can you even fucking imagine the headlines?" she said, getting more worked up by the second. "There goes all your high profile clients. No one wants a realtor from Kentucky who's fucking her stepbrother. The story pretty much writes itself. And people know we're sisters. God, Susannah Jethro's people would have a field day with that kind of a story. They've been dying to get their hands on some kind of dirt that could take me down."

"We didn't know," I said.

"I get that," Coco snapped. "But it has to end. Now. Our careers, everything we've worked so hard for, depends on it."

"Everything okay?" Wilder stepped out from the restaurant's awning.

Coco tossed her dark hair over her shoulder and softened her expression, hiding the emotions she'd just unleashed on me a second earlier. "Everything's fine, Wilder. I'll let you two *chat*."

The clicking of Coco's heels as she headed back inside were like a countdown until the moment we could finally be alone.

"Fuck." Wilder raked his fingers through his hair and then settled his hands on his hips, his weight shifting on his feet. "I didn't know, Addison. I swear to God."

"I believe you," I said, still finding it hard to look him in the eye. He was my stepbrother. My legal stepbrother. And I'd just sucked his cock that morning.

"You know I can't be with you now." I set fire to us, to our budding relationship, with eight little words. He stepped toward me, reaching for my arm. Our parents were mere feet away, enjoying their freshly delivered appetizers as our world was falling apart outside. "Don't."

"Why can't you be with me?" he asked. "Shit, Addison, you know how many times my dad has been married? You think this is going to last more than six months? I give it a year. Tops."

"They seem really happy." I drew in a sharp breath, watching my mom laugh at something Vince said. "I've never seen her so happy, Wilder."

"Fuck that." He pulled me to the other side of the awning, away from their view. "Stop looking at them. Look at me. I'm still the same person. I could give two shits about some fucking piece of bullshit paper that makes us related."

"It's not that simple." Coco's words echoed through my head. The implications of being with Wilder and what it could do to our careers were massive and undeniable.

"Addison, look at me," he said, pressing his body up against mine. He cupped the side of my face with his hand, but I pushed it away.

"We're in public," I said, my cheeks burning hot

as if the rest of the world knew our secret already. Suddenly the way he looked at me made me feel dirty instead of naughty, disgusting instead of sexy. "Don't do this."

"I don't see you as my stepsister. I didn't grow up with you. I don't have a history with you that spans beyond a month ago."

The faint scent of his expensive cologne surrounded us, enveloping me into a bubble reminiscent of the countless nights spent cultivating our torrid love affair. His lips caught my attention. Those full, beautiful, kissable lips, the ones I'd devoured and thought about nonstop, suddenly made my stomach churn.

If I forced myself to think about all the reasons I couldn't be with him, to reject his intense stares and disregard his convincing words, maybe it would make the pain of losing him more palatable.

"We should head back inside." I stepped away, only to be pulled right back against the brick façade of the building.

"I'm falling in love with you, Addison." A hint of a tremble in his voice, the first sign of weakness I'd ever seen in him, made my heart sink. His hand cupped my chin as he raked his thumb across my bottom lip. As he claimed my mouth one last time on the sidewalk outside the French bistro for all the world to see, my body held more nervous tension than I could stand. My eyes darted around the busy sidewalk as passersby looked at us.

A day ago, I'd have not cared. Funny how everything could change in an instant.

Wilder smirked. "Not even going to kiss me back, huh?"

"I-I can't," I said, my heart thumping hard in my ears. His revelation terrified me and made my insides burn hot with confusion all at the same time. "Besides, you don't love me, Wilder. You hardly know me."

"Don't tell me what I fucking feel. I know what I feel." His hand clenched into a ball as he beat it against his chest.

"We have to get back inside. They're going to know something's up. We've been out here a long time."

I peeled myself away from the brick wall and practically ran back inside, before he had a chance to talk me out of it or pull me into his arms again.

"Everything okay, sweetie?" my mom drawled. I'd never heard her ask such a thing before, but I supposed there was a first time for everything. Coco shot me a look, and I nodded in return.

"Everything's great, Mom." I pulled a napkin into my lap and stared down at my plate, the dish Wilder had apparently ordered for me against my wishes.

"Wilder thought you'd like that. What's it called again, Wilder?" my mom asked. She spoke to him as if they were pals, like they'd known each other for ages. Like she reveled in her newfound stepmother role. "Sweetie, you should thank him." She leaned into me. "He's really trying to make an effort here. Please be a good sport."

My blood boiled as I felt everyone's eyes on me. If they only knew the kind of skin I had in the game, maybe my behavior would make sense. I glanced at the diamond encrusted, rose gold watch on my wrist, the one Wilder had gifted me the weekend before when we went walking around our SoHo neighborhood and happened to pop into a jewelry boutique. "I really need to get going. I'm sorry. I have a showing tonight."

Tammy Lynn's face fell, and I spotted a hint of relief from Coco's end.

My mom stood up as I gathered my things. "Don't forget, sweetie, we're having a girls' day tomorrow.

We need to catch up. Maybe get our nails done?" She splayed her fingers. The diamond ring on her finger glittered.

"Yeah, fine, sounds good," I said as I hugged her. She squeezed me tight. Tighter than she'd ever done before, and I wasn't quite sure if it was her way to make up for all the years of being a shitty parent or if it was her way of telling me not to ruin this for her. Knowing Tammy Lynn, it was likely the latter.

"Nice meeting you, Vince." I nodded in his direction. Wilder's gaze burned holes right through me. "Wilder."

My mind took a snapshot of him, wishing I could replace it with one from that morning, before the shit storm happened. When we were two people who found love in an unsuspecting way and were navigating the murky waters of unbridled passion and vulnerability together.

I left the restaurant, opting to walk home in a feeble attempt to clear my head.

It didn't work.

The second I made it home, Wilder's wine-colored sweater was the first thing I saw, draped over the back of my arm chair. I pulled it over my head and curled up on the couch, breathing in his scent until it was no longer there and swallowing the hot, salty tears that tracked down my cheeks.

fourteen

WILDER

"So, son," my father said the next morning as we met for coffee. "What'd you think of the new family? Bet you never thought you'd be a big brother at your age, huh?" He chuckled as he took a sip from his steaming Styrofoam cup.

"Completely blindsided, if we're being honest."

"What do you think, though? You like 'em?" His brows were raised, almost begging me to tell him what he wanted to hear. The truth lingered on the tip of my tongue.

"I don't know, Dad." My lips pursed as I tried to fight it. It was no use. "This is what, number five? When does it end?"

"Oh, come on." My dad refused to remove his rose-colored glasses. "Tammy Lynn's different. She's not like the rest. She's a keeper."

He said that about Connie. And Debra. And the other two whose names escaped me. His marriage to my mother lasted maybe a decade. No marriage since had made it past the one-year mark.

"Wilder," he sighed. "Look. I'm not getting any younger. I want a companion. Someone to settle down with. I'll be retiring soon, and the nights get a little lonely. Not to mention I love Tammy Lynn. This marriage is forever, mark my words." He jammed his index finger into the table top. "Forever."

"Excuse me while I don't get too attached," I huffed, though he didn't seem to pick up on my sarcasm. He never was good at reading between the lines, and maybe that was why his marriages never lasted.

"What do you think of your new sisters? I know you're all grown adults, but maybe you can all try to spend a little time together after we leave? You're family now. You should know each other. Be there for each other."

"I don't know about Coco. She seems to have a stick up her ass," I said. "But that Addison. What a looker, am I right?"

I tested him, though he was so dense he'd never know it. His face turned a shade of crimson, his smile washing away. "Wilder, don't speak that way about your sister."

"Kind of hard to be sitting across the table from one of the most beautiful women I've ever seen and think of her as my sister," I said, taking a careful sip of coffee. "I'm an adult. She's an adult. Things happen…"

My father went to speak, but the words appeared to all jumble before they had a chance to make it out of his mouth. He was flustered, and Vince Van Cleef never got flustered. He was a smooth-talking salesman. A guy's guy and a lady's man all rolled into one. He had a comment for everything and could talk his way out of any situation. But me talking about the hotness of my new stepsister got him all kinds of flustered.

"You won't speak about Addison that way," Vince growled like he did when I was a troubled teenager. I knew that tone all too well. My mother shipped me off to stay with him every summer until I turned eighteen, hoping I'd come back a reformed man. It never worked. It wasn't until she died, that I was forced to grow up and change my trouble-seeking ways. "Do you understand me?"

I shook my head and stared out the window. The city was one giant all-you-could-eat buffet of beautiful women, many of them passing by in their Burberry coats and Manolo heels with their exotic good looks. But none of them held a candle to Addison.

It was only a matter of time before Tammy Lynn was ancient history, a blip on the timeline of Vince Van Cleef's life. And yet I had to suffer. I had to let the woman I loved go so that my love-addicted father could stick his dick in something that made him feel special for a year of his pathetic life.

My mind wandered to dark corners, imagining what could happen in a year from now. I imagined bumping into Addison out and about, seeing her on the arm of some new guy. I imagined his hands cupping her face and his cock buried in her tight pussy. The one that belonged to me. The one she let me own. The one I never intended on letting go of, no matter how hard things got.

Addison was my one in seven fucking billion.

"Wilder, I'm talking to you," my father's voice boomed. "I said, do you understand me?"

I nodded in an attempt to pacify him, though I didn't understand him at all. No one did. All I understood, and all I'd ever understood, was that Vince Van Cleef was a selfish asshole.

"Anyway," he said. "I was going to talk to you about this little real estate venture I've been working on. There's a network of timeshares in Boca Raton that I think will…"

I let him drone on about some surefire timeshare deal. It would "only" cost two million dollars and he'd do all the legwork. All I had to do was plunk down a bit of cold hard cash, which he insisted was pocket change for me.

I stared down into the bottom of my coffee cup as he continued. It seemed he only ever contacted me when he wanted money or some kind of assistance anymore anyway. At fifty-five years old, Vince Van Cleef had lived a dozen different lives and had not a damn thing to show for himself. He strolled around town, cruising from showing to showing in his 1998 Boston green BMW Z-3 like he was reliving his glory days when the market was hot and women threw themselves at him.

It was all a façade.

I didn't know much about Tammy Lynn other than the fact that Addison didn't say a whole lot about her. I knew she'd been married just as often as my dad, and that she didn't seem too involved in Addison's life, but I was certain she deserved better than Vince. Most women did.

"So, what do you say, son?" My dad used his best loving father voice. "About the investment?"

fifteen

addison

I yanked the door open to the day spa Coco had picked and was immediately ushered to a changing room and outfitted with a robe and slippers. Moments later, I was escorted to a private room where my mother and sister were already sipping cucumber-infused waters as attendants kneaded and tugged their hands like bread dough.

"This is the life," my mother sighed. "Oh, gosh, I needed this."

Coco and I exchanged looks, quietly amused at my mother pretending to have a stressful life. Her simple, small town life in Darlington, Kentucky working in a real estate office paled in comparison to the stress we put ourselves through to make something of ourselves. But we said nothing, like the good daughters we were.

"So, how exciting is it that you have a brother now?" My mom beamed. "And he lives here in the city! I mean, if you ever wanted to spend time with him, catch a bite to eat, need help hanging a picture—whatever—I'm sure Wilder would be there in an instant. He seems like a good boy."

I hated that she talked about him as if he were a child, like the friendly neighborhood boy scout always willing to lend a helping hand or help an old lady carry her groceries inside.

Wilder was so much more than she knew, and he was so much more than I could ever explain. The pain of separating myself from him and attempting to drown out the thickness of the emotions that weighed heavily on my heart only served as fuel to the fire of resentment that'd burned in me for so long.

I resented my mother.

And now, I almost hated her.

Though I supposed it wasn't fair. It wasn't like she knew. She didn't do anything on purpose. But it was the fact that she could con anyone in the world into marrying her. Why'd it have to be Vince?

"I'd like to leave my ring on," she said to the masseuse. "I can't stop looking at it. It's so nice being married again." She shrugged her shoulders and flashed a coy, dimpled grin, as if it were her first time as a newlywed. "So, Dakota, how're things with Harrison?"

"They're still living together," I interjected.

"When are you going to cut the cord?" Mom asked, shaking her head as if she truly gave a damn. It was all an act. It always was. "I'd love to see you meet someone new. I want to see that sparkle in those big, blue eyes of yours again."

Coco rolled her eyes. "Who has time to date? Certainly not me. And who wants to date a woman who could be flown clear across the country at a moment's notice?"

Coco and Harrison worked out well for a while since he was her producer. He flew wherever she did. They were both obsessed with their work and obsessed with each other, until shit got real. Coco still refused to talk about what really happened, which only told me it was bad.

"You know that boy you used to date in high school, the country singer guy, what's his name again?" Mom scrunched her face, pretending like she didn't remember. The whole world knew his name. Beau Mason was the biggest country rock singer in the history of music, with more platinum albums in the last decade than most recording legends had in their lifetimes.

"Beau." Coco said his name through gritted teeth. She'd refused to talk about him in the nearly ten years that had passed since they went their separate ways.

"Yes! Beau Mason." My mom smiled fondly, as if she had nothing but good memories of him. I barely remembered Beau since I was a little younger than her when they were together, but he was my sister's first taste of real love. And her first taste of real heartbreak. Those things never leave you, no matter how much time passes. "You know, I heard he was retiring. For good. Can you believe that? He's been so successful and he just wants to give it all up for a quiet life back home."

"Good for him." Coco rolled her eyes. It was the

most she'd said about him in years. If you asked me, she was still wildly in love with him. She'd never admit it though, and she refused to listen to any of his songs.

"Maybe he's not happy," I said. I glanced across the room at my sister, and I could've sworn she was trying to blink away tears. I wanted to tell her she didn't have to be such a diamond all the time, sparkly and pretty and flawless on the outside and so hard that no one could break her on the inside. It was okay to be vulnerable sometimes. "Maybe he's searching for something else. Someone else…"

Coco shot me a look that silenced my commentary. "You know, Addison was seeing someone recently."

"You were?" My mom seemed shocked. "Please tell me you're back with that nice Kyle boy." She didn't know the half of what went down with Kyle, and I never quite had the energy to share it with her.

"Nope, not Kyle." I shot Coco a look. We were even.

The spa attendants ushered us into another room, where three massage tables were set up.

"Oh, gosh, I just love a good massage," Mom

drawled. "Vince tries to rub my shoulders, bless his heart, but he just doesn't do it the way a professional can."

I preferred my massages to be quiet and tranquil, but with Tammy Lynn's inability to sit in silence for too long, it wasn't going to happen that day. I breathed in the eucalyptus oil diffusing beneath me and settled into the soft cushion of the table as I tried to tune her out.

"Oh, girls!" my mom's excited voice was muffled through the headrest of the massage table. "I forgot to tell you, Vince and I are planning a family vacation. We're thinking sunny Florida! He's going to rent us a house right on Cocoa Beach. For one week. All five of us. One, big happy family. How's that sound?"

Like torture. Like pure fucking torture.

"Mom, I can't take off work," I objected. I couldn't be around Wilder for seven days. Not when the wound was so fresh. Peeling myself from him had left a mark, and spending a week with him in Florida was going to be like picking the scab. "I'd have to talk to Brenda. I don't know…"

"Same here," Coco added. "I'd have to clear it with the network. I can't make any promises."

Mom was silent. Muffled sniffles echoed in the

tiny room we shared. She was crying. In true Tammy Lynn form, she managed to make us feel like shit for not giving her what she wanted. She'd done it all our lives.

"It would really," she said between sniffles, "mean a lot if you could try."

I groaned. Maybe if I was lucky, Wilder wouldn't go. "I'll try, Mom. When were you thinking?"

"Vince is still working out the details. We were thinking next month sometime. Would that give you girls enough time to plan?" Gone were the sniffles and woe-is-me act. She seemed happy again.

Maybe she really did want us to be a big, happy family. Maybe she really did love Vince. Maybe he really did make her happy. And maybe he was going to be the one person to bring out the best in her—the person Coco and I always dreamed she would be.

* * *

"Girls, this means so much to me," Mom said as we left the spa later that morning. "You have no idea." Her eyes began to water as her peppy façade faded. "I know I wasn't the best mother, but I want to make it up to you. And I know you never knew your father, but Vince is willing to step in. It's a little late in life, but he wants to be there for you. We both want to make this family work. And it means so much to me to have your support."

Coco and I exchanged looks, practically reading each other's thoughts. Was this another act? Did she mean it? Was she really turning over a new leaf?

"Love you, Mom," Coco said, wrapping an arm around her before I followed suit.

"Vince and I will be in the city a few more days," she said. "If you want to get together again, just let me know. He's got a few sights he wants to show me, some special evenings planned. But I'd like to see you girls again before we leave. You never come home anymore."

It was true. We avoided Darlington like the plague, especially Coco.

"Anyway, I'll let you know about Florida," she said, plastering a smile on her face. "I can't wait."

Mom hailed a cab as Coco and I walked off in the other direction, waiting until we were far enough away to start dissecting our morning with Tammy Lynn.

"So that was… fun," Coco said as we briskly headed south from Midtown.

"She seems happy."

"She always seems that way. Give it more time. As soon as the newness wears off, she'll be airing all their dirty laundry and filing for divorce. You know the drill."

"This one seems different though, Co."

She shrugged. "Honestly, I don't have the time nor the energy to give two shits about mom's love life anymore. It's exhausting, and we're grown now. It's no longer our concern."

"Easy for you to say." My phone buzzed in my pocket. I didn't have to look at it to know who it was. He'd been messaging me all morning, begging me to come over so we could talk. I pulled my phone out to read his latest appeal.

"Oh, my God." Coco glanced over my shoulder and read the text. "I thought you were going to end it with him."

"I am. He's just having a hard time accepting that we're done," I lied. I was having just as hard of a time as he was.

"End it, Addison." Coco shoved her hands in the pockets of her skinny jeans as her stiletto boots clicked on the pitted cement. She could be cold and hard sometimes, like frozen concrete.

I wanted to tell her it wasn't that simple. It wasn't going to happen overnight. I almost told her I wasn't sure I was strong enough to walk away from the best thing that had ever happened to me. Instead I gave her my best "I'm working on it" before saying goodbye and heading straight for Wilder's apartment.

* * *

My first words when I saw him were, "This has to stop."

My body wholeheartedly disagreed, though.

I wanted to throw myself onto him, wrap my legs around his body, and fall softly into the comfort of his soft bed sheets. I wanted to feel him deep inside me, taste him, smell him, lose myself in him.

But I didn't do any of that.

I imagined there was an alternate universe somewhere where the two of us were laughing and playing like two carefree lovers. Addison and Wilder were living their happily-ever-after fairytale romance somewhere, just not in the here and now.

"Get your hot little ass in here, now," he growled in the low, sexy voice that instantly made my panties melt.

He's your stepbrother!

He led me inside as the elevator doors closed behind me and pushed me up against the wall of his foyer. He leaned down and took my bottom lip between his teeth. Wilder was never that aggressive, and I supposed the thought of losing me for good had done a number on him. Maybe it'd made him hungrier for me?

I teetered between giving myself to him one final time and standing my ground. "I mean it. We can't do this."

"No," he seethed. His breath quickened, forcing itself in and out of his nostrils like a raging bull. "I love you, Addison. I fucking love you. I'm not letting you go. You're mine."

His hands flew to the sides of my face, holding it still as he forced another kiss on my lips.

"I don't think of you as my stepsister. You're not. You're my girlfriend. You're the only person in this whole fucked up world who gets me."

I didn't recognize the man standing before me, the man clinging so desperately to me like a shipwrecked sailor clinging to a sinking lifeboat. Wilder backed away from me, running a hand through his hair and tugging on the ends. His bloodshot eyes suggested maybe he hadn't slept the night before, though I couldn't blame him. I hadn't, either.

I was better at hiding those kinds of things. I'd become a polished rock on the outside, able to hide the imperfections deep inside me so no one could see when I was broken. When all I wanted to do was crumble into pieces, the rest of the world saw a girl who appeared to have her shit together. I was a fraud.

"Look at me and tell me you feel nothing," he demanded.

My bottom lip trembled. I said the words in my head first, as if I needed to practice them. They were a lie, and I knew that. "I feel nothing."

His aqua eyes glassed over. "I don't believe you. Two days ago, you were mine. Now you feel nothing. Fucking liar."

My heart ached for him. For me. For us. "I don't have a choice, Wilder. Being with you has certain implications. Not just for me, but for everyone. My mom. Your dad. My sister."

"Oh, so now you're a fucking martyr, Addison? What, you think you need to sacrifice your happiness, your life, so everyone else is happy?"

"I'm not a selfish person, Wilder."

He rushed up, his body like a force field that backed me up against the wall once again without even touching me. With his mouth mere inches from mine, I wasn't sure if he wanted to kiss me or bite me or both. "You're a goddamn saint, Addison, and that's your fucking problem. What do you want? Huh? What does Addison Andrews want?"

My mouth hung open, silently begging for him to quiet my thoughts with his lips. It worked before, it would work again. I knew it. If he kissed me, nothing else would matter, if only temporarily. Beneath my polished exterior, I was a weak woman. I couldn't be an unbreakable diamond like my sister. "I want you."

I stared at the marled pattern of the stained concrete floors and hung my head, as if declaring my true feeling sucked the life out of me. Wilder's hand angled under my jaw, lifting my mouth to his and breathing life back into my exhausted soul one kiss at a time. Unapologetic love rained down on me as the heat of his body made the outside world fade away. He hoisted me up around his waist as he carried me back to his room, laying me gently on his bed.

My mind begged for him to stop, and it was only after we were both naked that I realized my body had won that war. His hands traced my naked flesh as his tongue tasted my arousal. I was his once again. The fight was stacked from the start.

I'd have to throw in the towel another day.

I couldn't do it.

Not yet.

sixteen

WILDER

I pulled myself out of her and crawled beside her, laying my head on the pillow and widening my arms. She always slinked up next to me when we were finished, and while I wasn't big on cuddling, I always secretly enjoyed the way she tucked herself against me.

Addison pulled away, rolling herself toward the edge of the bed.

She climbed out and fished around on the floor for her clothes, redressing as fast as she could.

"Where're you going?" I sat up, watching her

beautiful body disappear behind an armor of designer clothing.

"I shouldn't have done that. I shouldn't have given myself to you." She turned to look at me, her face taut.

I slid off the bed and grabbed my jeans off the floor, stepping into them as she headed toward the door. "Addison, wait. Where are you going?"

"I'm really sorry. I sent the wrong message."

She reached for the door, but I slammed my fist against it, holding it shut with the weight of my body. "Let's talk, all right? We can figure this out. There's got to be a solution."

Her full lips formed a hard line across her pretty face. "Believe me, Wilder, if there was a way to make this work, I'd be all over it. I stayed up all night last night thinking about it. About you. Us. If anyone found out about us being together, now that you're my stepbrother, it would destroy my career. My sister's career. You can hide behind your corporation. You're a nameless face behind a generic LLC. I am my own brand. So is Coco. We can't throw away everything we've ever worked for to become known as a couple of backwoods Kentucky hicks who sleep with family members."

"How would anyone know?" I scratched my head. "Who the fuck would know about our parents being married, and why would anyone care?"

"You'd be surprised what people can find if they dig hard enough. There are people out there who aren't very happy that Coco is about to replace Susannah Jethro. And there are people who'd kill to have her spot and would love nothing more than a reason to take her down. And everyone in this city knows I'm her sister. She goes down, I do too."

"So that's it, then?"

"What choice do I have?" Her shoulders slumped, her blue eyes staring the ground as she blinked away tears. "You act like this is easy for me."

My hand fell from the door. "Looks like you've made up your mind."

Our eyes met as her lips parted, and I waited for her to speak, but nothing came out. There was only one possible thing she could say to make any of this better, and I knew deep down she didn't have the guts.

"Go." Pain settled in the base of my throat as I pulled the door open for her.

She drew in a deep breath and wiped the corner of her eye with the back of her hand. "I'll send you some new agent referrals, if you'd like."

"You fucking kidding me?" My hands flew to my temples, letting the door slam upon my release. "You're breaking my fucking heart right now, and you want to talk business? God, I knew you were hot and cold when I met you, but this is really fucking pathetic, Addison. Guess it's a good thing I found out now how frozen you are inside. Just flip a switch. It's all about your fucking career."

"I was trying to be polite." Her voice was weak and thin and lacked her signature confidence. "Regardless of all of this, I know you still have a business to run."

"Were you trying to be polite when you were riding my cock ten minutes ago?"

Addison's lips trembled, making me realize I'd been yelling. I hated that I'd made her cry. I hated talking to her like that, but all I saw was red. I hadn't felt this way since Nikki, and I sure as hell didn't think Addison would remotely come close to the same category as that bitch.

"You know what? I'm going to keep you as my agent. You know why? Because I fucking give a damn about you. I don't know why I do after all this, but I do.

So I'm going to let you keep me on as a client so your dream of being the top agent in the city can come true.

"And when you reach the top, you're going to realize it wasn't half as great as you thought it was going to be. You're going to show me every goddamn apartment in all of Manhattan. You're going to have to see me every single week. And I'm going to serve as a constant reminder of what might have been. What you walked away from. The only guy who ever knew the real you and who loved you in spite of the fucked up flaws you try so damn hard to hide."

Addison constantly projected an image to the outside world. The shoes she wore. The bags she carried. The way she held her head up high and flashed her million-dollar smile no matter how empty she felt inside. When she was with me, stripped and naked and vulnerable, I saw the real her. The one with insecurities and issues, just like everyone else. The one with a past she tried her hardest to escape. And I loved her in spite of it all.

Perfection bored me. Flawlessness was shallow. I loved the real Addison, the woman she was on the inside. The way she looked with no makeup and messy hair. The way she slinked around when she was relaxed. Her authentic self filled me with a newfound realization that maybe not everyone in this world was an asshole. Authenticity wasn't dead, after all.

I hated texting because it made me feel so disconnected from the world. It was funny how such a simple technological advance could cause such intense feelings of loneliness, but I couldn't help the way I felt. Addison restored the interpersonal human connection I'd been missing all those years, filling the gaping hole I once thought could be fixed by a stupid rule.

"What if I decide to release you as a client?" she asked.

"You won't," I sneered. "You won't because you're too driven. You want that top spot, and you're going to do whatever it takes to get it, even if it means dying a little bit inside every time you see me."

"So, you're punishing me?" She wiped her tears once more. "That's what you're doing, isn't it?"

The little life she'd worked so hard to perfect and keep in control was quickly burning to the ground. She wasn't in control of a damn thing anymore. I almost felt sorry for her.

"Leave," I seethed. "Now."

* * *

A week passed, and then another, and while I may have calmed down a bit, the wound was still fresh and gaping, oozing with every step I took around the city that could only be described as ours.

The streets we'd walked together. The coffee shops and boutiques we'd stopped into on lazy Sundays. Central Park. Every square inch of my apartment her naked little ass had touched. The favorite sweater of mine she'd climb into when the nights got too cold. Her side of the bed. My skin. My hair. She was in everything I touched, making me lovesick with every breath I took.

I burned my sheets in a metal bucket on the roof of my building. It was a drastic move. I thought it'd make me feel better or it'd be symbolic, or some shit like that. It only fueled the fire raging deep in my soul.

I checked my phone on my walk home from the office. A missed call from Lainey McQuinn, a girl I used to casually date off and on the year before. My hurt ran deep, and I was only a man.

"Lainey," I said as I returned her call, pleasantly surprised at the fact that she remembered my no texting rule. I forced pleasantness into my voice, shoving the dark thoughts and crippling pain into the back of my mind. "Haven't heard from you in a while. What's going on?"

"Hey, Wilder baby," she cooed in her thick, Brooklyn accent. Lainey was a modern-day sexpot. Or at least she was last time I saw her with her shapely runner's legs up to her eyeballs and fiery red hair that contrasted against flawless, milky white skin. She was always more than happy to be on standby during those lonely nights post-Nikki. "I went to a dinner party at Graze Central last night. Reminded me of that time, um, we went into the bathroom… and…"

"I remember," I said, mentally replaying a bathroom quickie we'd had in the middle of a boring group dinner.

"Was just thinkin' about you, was all," she said. I knew damn well what she meant. "I think about you from time to time, you know. Usually when I'm bored… at night… in my bed…"

"You home?" I didn't need to read between the lines any longer. She wanted to fuck, and I wanted to get Addison out of my system.

"Yeah, why?"

"I'm coming over."

* * *

"Hey, stranger." Lainey leaned against her open door, resting her head against the wood as a sultry grin spread across her lips. Her tongue traced her upper lip the second our eyes met. "Been a long time. Come in."

She stepped aside, her low cut top revealing the subtle bounce of her cleavage with each movement. Tight jeans hugged her long legs and round ass, and blazing curls framed her face. Eyes like two vivid emeralds twinkled against the late afternoon sun as she failed to contain her excitement.

"Nice to see you," she said, shutting the door behind me. "Hadn't heard from you in a while. Didn't know if you finally met a nice girl and settled down, or somethin'."

I took a seat on her sofa, the one I'd fucked her on a few times years back. I thought seeing her would ignite the part of me who used sex as an escape, but all I saw was Addison.

Lainey sauntered over to the sofa, stepping between it and the coffee table until she was straddling my legs. Lowering herself into my lap, a fog of her signature Juicy Couture perfume enveloped us, and I found myself mourning the classic Chanel No. 5 Addison used to strategically dab behind her ears and in the crook of her elbows. It wasn't much, but it was just enough for me to appreciate whenever I devoured her.

The warmth of Lainey's lips as they pressed against my forehead sent my body into a state of rigor. My hands, which should've been halfway up her shirt by then, were paralyzed at my side. My cock hadn't a single throb.

Fuck.

Even though I wasn't with Addison anymore, my body and soul and all that I was still belonged to her and only her. Not even no-strings-attached sex with Lainey McQuinn could make me forget the pain.

I gently pushed her off my lap. "Fuck, Lainey. I'm sorry. I can't do this."

"What the hell is your problem?" She crossed her arms, brow furrowed.

"I'm sorry." There was nothing more to say, and it sure as hell wasn't anything I needed to talk to her about. Bolting for the door, I got the hell out of there.

seventeen

addison

I paced the dated kitchen of a musty, abandoned apartment building, checking my watch every other minute. I'd received a tip on a building about to hit the market, and like the good agent I was, notified Wilder immediately and scheduled a showing.

We hadn't seen each other nor spoken in two weeks. Two very long, excruciating weeks. I tried to lose myself in running and work, and any free time I had was spent following Coco around like a lost puppy or organizing and re-organizing my closet. Coco assured me I had done the right thing for everyone involved, and she let me cry on her shoulder every night that first week.

"The scars will always be there," she'd said as she rubbed my back, her voice distant as if she were recalling her own pain. "No denying that. But with time, it won't hurt as much."

A knock on the door made my heart fall flat on the floor. Straightening my shoulders and bracing myself, I let him in. Dressed in an Italian silk suit with a bold red tie and polished shoes, he offered me a cordial nod as he stepped past, his cold, uninviting demeanor a far cry from the man falling apart at the seams just two weeks ago.

"So, this hits the market tomorrow," I said, getting right down to business and praying the overwhelming urge to talk about us would dissipate. "There are nine units as well as retail space at ground level. It's currently being occupied by a longtime tenant, as I'm sure you already noticed."

His hands in his pockets, he went from room to room in the small, one-bedroom apartment, saying nothing.

"There are five studios, three one-bedroom units,

and one two-bedroom unit," I added, following him, yet keeping a careful distance. "Seller insists all units are up to code mechanically. He was in the middle of renovating the building and ran into some money problems, so that should give us plenty of leverage if you want to move quick on this. I'd suggest and all cash offer and a three-day close. That's assuming you want the place."

I flipped a light switch, and the room lit up for three seconds before the bulb popped and burnt out.

"Place needs a lot of work. No denying that. We'll demand an inspection, of course," I continued, silently willing him to speak. His quietude ate away at me second by second. "The location couldn't be better. I mean, units like this, at this price, don't come around often."

Wilder turned on his heel, walking up to me with a steady cadence. "I really need you to stop talking right now."

My lips sealed at his demand and the heaviness in my chest weighed me down. He never used to speak to me that way. I knew he was hurting, but he had to know I was too.

He turned away, heading into the bathroom of the unit and inspecting drawers and fixtures. Normally I'd have told him the water was turned off or that I knew of a guy who remodeled bathrooms at a discount, but I kept my mouth shut just as he'd asked.

We headed back to the kitchen where my bag waited on the dusty Formica countertop.

"I'll think about this and let you know." His lifeless aqua eyes avoided mine as he raked his palm across the hint of a five o'clock shadow lining his chiseled jaw.

I nodded, scared to breathe a word that might set him off. We lingered in the stillness of the vacated apartment for a moment before I took the first step away from him, ignoring his penetrating stare. But by the time I reached the door, it was too much. I couldn't leave like that.

"I'm hurting too, you know." I winced, though he didn't see it. My back toward him, I was too terrified to turn around. "I miss you every second of every day."

Giving him a few seconds to respond, my heart sunk when I realized he wasn't going to say anything. With an unsteady hand twisting the black iron doorknob, I stepped out into the hall, picking up the key box from the floor and waiting for him to leave.

By the time he emerged, he made a beeline for the

stairs, saying nothing. A teasing whisper of his cologne breezed by as he walked away, lingering as I listened to the fade of his footsteps. A couple weeks ago we were lovers, tackling this bullshit called life together.

Now he hated me.

* * *

I kicked off my heels and dug my aching feet into the soft rug by my front door. Seeing Wilder that morning had left me a mess of scattershot emotions, disabling me from uttering a complete sentence for the remainder of the afternoon. I was in the midst of cancelling my afternoon appointments, something I'd never done before, when Skylar brought me a handful of chocolates.

"You all right?" she'd asked me after I returned from showing Wilder the unit on 86th Street. "You don't seem like yourself lately."

I peered up into her round, doe eyes, the eyes of a fresh college graduate who probably lived her life one selfie and social engagement at a time, and I longed for an ounce of her naïveté.

"I'm fine," I lied, sweeping the chocolates off my desk and into the palm of my hand where they began to melt. "Just tired." That part was true. I hadn't been sleeping well the last couple weeks. Cold bed sheets and an ache in my heart that couldn't be ignored made it impossible. I popped a couple pieces of the candy into my mouth, but I couldn't taste them.

I cut out of the office early and headed straight home, fully intending on drowning my pain in an overflowing glass of red wine and the hottest bubble bath I could possibly stand; the kind I'd have to slowly lower myself into one inch at a time; the kind that scalded my skin into a painful shade of raw pink. I needed to hurt on the outside to numb the hurt on the inside.

But no sooner had I kicked off my heels than there was a knock on my door. I glanced at my watch. It was maybe three o'clock, and I wasn't expecting a delivery. Standing up on my toes, I squinted through the peephole.

Wilder.

He must have seen me walking home.

I smoothed my hair flat and pulled the door open. He was still in the suit from that morning, the one with the angry red tie.

"Hi?"

"Did you mean it?"

"Mean what?"

"You think about me every moment of every day?"

I nodded, shrinking half my body behind the door. Our eyes met, and I couldn't look away no matter how hard I tried. Before I realized what I was saying, I found myself muttering, "You can come in, if you want."

He brushed past me, our shoulders grazing just enough to send a current of livewire down my side, and I shut the door behind him.

"I meant all of it," I said, clasping my hand across my chest and digging my fingers into the flesh of my neck. "It's not the same since…"

"Since you walked away." He finished my sentence in such a way that I knew he was still the Wilder from that morning, the one still so ripe with hurt he could hardly look at me without flaring his nostrils. His hands rested on his hips, and the glint of his belt buckle caught the late afternoon sun that trickled through the curtains of my dim apartment. It was still daylight outside, but inside we stood in a whole different world, a darker world where we weren't supposed to be together. But being together was the only thing that might save us.

"I don't know what to do." My voice broke and my mind was a flurry of all the thoughts I'd been thinking the last two weeks. I imagined the look on Coco's face if we were to get back together. I imagined the heartbreak it would cause my mother. I imagined my reputation as a realtor crumbling to rubble as my competitors flung ruthless nicknames and rumors in my direction.

Wilder lunged at me, pinning me against the door with the magnitude of his intense stare. Hot tears stung my eyes, blurring my vision as I attempted to fight them off. All I wanted was for him to kiss me. I remembered what it felt like, but I was beginning to forget. Each day that passed pushed that sensory memory further and further away, like a dream I'd had weeks ago and I was beginning to forget the details. I needed him to look at me the way he used to and not like I was some kind of horrible monster. I was falling apart, and only his love would save me.

"Stop talking," he commanded. His hands found my hips, and his fingers dug into my skin as if he were holding tight and incapable of letting me go. My eyes closed. Tears streamed down my cheeks. A warmth against my lips, like the kind I dreamt of every night, ignited a spark inside me.

He kissed me.

And the kiss was soft and tender, not angry or bitter. His right hand left my side and trailed up to the side of my cheek, delicately cupping my face as his lips worked mine apart. Our tongues danced, and the taste of him set me on fire. I'd craved him; his touch, his taste, his scent. Convinced that I was dreaming it all up, I refused to open my eyes.

His left hand traveled down my side until it found the hem of my skirt. He hiked it up to the top of my thighs before slipping his hand between them and tugging my silk panties to the side. One finger passed between my folds as he found the innermost part of me. Wilder slipped one finger inside, followed by a second, curling them toward him and stroking me, long and gentle, slow and meaningful, as if he were trying to savor our time together. His fingers filled me while his lips worked mine.

I didn't even try to stop it. I'd willed this. I'd fantasized about it every single night for two weeks. I'd dreamt of him nightly and cried myself awake from a deep slumber more times than I cared to admit.

Wilder removed his hand from my wetness and ripped my panties off. Soft, lace-covered shreds tickled my skin as he tugged them down, but I didn't care. With my eyes still clenched tight, I heard the clinking of his belt buckle. My heart pounded hard in my chest. I just wanted the emptiness to go away. I wanted to feel every inch of him inside me.

The sensation of his hand freeing his erection from his pants and positioning it at my entrance as my legs gripped his sides sent an ache straight to my core. But the second he entered me, the heavy, burdening pain dissipated into thin air. Like it was never there in the first place. With my arms draped over his shoulders, I gave myself to him.

But did it matter? I was his anyway.

The raw awareness of his unsheathed cock coupled with the fact that none of that was supposed to be happening made every thrust a thousand times more intense than I ever dreamed possible. At least I was on the pill, though I don't think it'd have changed anything. I wanted him more than anything, and my body was willing to go into self-destruct mode to get it.

My teeth grazed over my bottom lip as I stifled a moan. I didn't want to look at him. I didn't want to know if he was looking at me with deep longing or unforgivable hatred. It felt like love, the way he was fucking me, but it was easier to pretend everything was fine if I didn't have to see his face. I easily replaced it with the way I saw him in my memory: strong and resilient with mischief in his eyes. Crazy about me.

My lower back ached as every thrust forced it to rub against the wood of the door, but none of that mattered. The physical pain on the outside was miniscule compared to what was going on inside me. My body and heart worked in tandem to soak in every detail of that moment from the smell of the cologne that faintly floated from the collar of his white shirt to the way his hair felt as I gripped the back of his neck. My mind quieted itself, as if to graciously give us all a break.

Wilder groaned as he released himself inside me and I let go, riding an intense wave of all-consuming pleasure as my hips bucked wildly in response to his writhing cock.

When it was all over, he pulled out of me and I slid down the wall, my knees buckling and threatening to give out. I needed someone, or something, to cling onto before I crumpled.

I forced my eyes open, looking at him for the first time since he'd kissed me, the memory of which would forever be burned into my lips. I drank him in, starting with the two pools of blue staring into my soul. He was real. He was there. He'd just fucked me. And I had loved every second of it.

Emptiness infiltrated my spirit once again as I accepted the fact that he was no longer a part of me. I tugged my skirt down my thighs and straightened my blouse. I dared myself to speak, but I chickened out.

His buckled his pants while tears filled my eyes once again. I wanted to go back to the way we were. I wanted to smile again. I wanted to wake up next to him every morning and rush home from a long day of work and happily lose myself in a tangled web of sheets and sex. I wanted his fingers in my hair and his mouth owning every square inch of real estate on my naked body.

Uncontrollable tears pooled in my eyes before trailing down my cheeks and splashing in tiny drops on the tops of my bare feet. I couldn't stop them if I tried. I wanted to be with him, but no amount of desire or secret fuck sessions would ever change the reality of our situation.

Wilder left my presence and returned moments later with a handful of tissues, dabbing my cheeks. How ironic that I was the one who'd hurt him so badly, and yet there he was, wiping my tears.

I didn't deserve him and yet I needed him more than I needed the air I breathed. I stumbled to the living room, falling into the overstuffed chair and burying my face in my arm. My shoulders heaved with every sob that escaped my mouth, but my face stayed hidden. I didn't want him to see me like that, and I couldn't look at him again.

"This has to be the last time," I sobbed. "This can't happen again."

His silence killed me. Absolutely killed me. I needed to know what he was thinking, but then again, none of it would've made a difference.

There was only one solution to all of this: I had to fall out of love with him.

"Please, just go," I hiccupped into my arm.

Silence.

I felt him, just mere feet from me. He lingered for a second. And then I listened as the soles of his shoes echoed toward the door. I didn't look up again until I'd heard it slam behind him. He was only doing what I'd asked, but it didn't keep my heart from shattering into countless slivers that ached with every beat.

eighteen

WILDER

There's a certain kind of power in words unspoken. Which was why I said nothing the entire time I was fucking my stepsister.

Stepsister. The word is such a fucking joke when

you're a grown man. It conjures up an image of a bratty, pig-tailed, pimple-faced little girl who chases you around and tries to annoy you. You're forced to live together like one picture-perfect family as your parents pretend you're blood related. You take family vacations and do your best to get along, creating memories you'll someday laugh about when you're all grown.

But I didn't have that experience with her. Not a damn bone in my body saw her in any kind of sisterly way. We didn't have a history—not like that, anyway.

I'd spotted her walking home around three that afternoon, and I recognized the pained look on her face. It was the exact same one I'd been wearing since I saw her that morning. So I followed her. I wanted to know if she meant what she said.

It wasn't my intention to fuck her up against a wall and bury myself balls deep inside her as she cried and wordlessly begged for more. In a way it was fucked up on both our parts, and there weren't any words that would've made any kind of sense out of what we did.

So I said nothing. It was better that way. She needed to feel my love, not hear about it. I could give her a million reasons as to why we could—why we should—try to make it work, but none would hold a flame to the way my body spoke to hers when we were together.

As far as I was concerned, she knew how I felt. I wasn't afraid to face our strange predicament head on and take what belonged to me. But I wasn't going to chase her around like some pathetic, pining jackass.

The ball was in her court.

* * *

The following afternoon, I headed to tour another dilapidated building Addison had emailed me about that morning. I checked my email and spouted off the address to my driver and within twenty minutes, he dropped me off in front of an abandoned warehouse in China Town.

I headed inside, my heart squeezing tight with each step I took. I'd done a little research on the property when she told me about the listing, but it wasn't the property I was interested in that day. I just wanted to see her again.

My mouth twitched into a smile as I thought about what she'd probably do. Knowing Addison, she'd act all professional and pretend like nothing happened, and then she'd nonchalantly slink her body a certain way or step into my space and quietly plead for me to take her again.

Fine. If that was what she wanted, that was what I'd give to her. I had no problem fucking her in secret and biding my time until our parents' eventual divorce.

I yanked the door open to the warehouse office, clearing my throat before stepping inside.

"Mr. Van Cleef." A young blonde with stacked tits spilling from her shirt and makeup-caked eyes sat perched on an abandoned desk. She rose and popped her hand out to offer a shake. If her top were any lower, the pink of her nipples would've been showing. "Hi, I'm Skylar. I'm Ms. Andrews' assistant. She's really sorry. She couldn't make it, so she sent me. I hope that's all right."

A wide grin plastered across the lower half of her face as she tried to hide her attraction toward me. Young women like her were horrible at hiding that shit. She couldn't take her eyes off me, walking a little too close as we left the office and rambling on like a nervous, giddy schoolgirl.

With an armful of paperwork about the listing, she blathered on about the property like a complete amateur, stumbling over certain real estate terms. If Addison didn't want to see me, she could've at least sent someone with half a brain and a little bit of experience to fill in.

"I'm sorry, where did you say Addison was?" I interrupted her.

Skylar's eyes flew to the left as her brows scrunched, almost as if she wasn't expecting that question and had to search for an excuse on the spot. She swept her bleach blonde hair over her shoulder and popped her chest out. "I think she had another appointment? Maybe. I don't know."

"You're her assistant," I said, stepping back. "You don't know her schedule?"

"I think something came up." Skylar forced a nervous smile as she twirled her hair between two manicured fingers. Her big brown eyes looked me up and down as if I were some guy she was meeting for drinks and a casual fuck. She probably didn't even realize she was doing it.

"Don't bullshit me here." I paced toward the door. "I'm sorry, Skylar. This isn't about you. I have to go."

"But wait," she called, her heels clicking on the industrial floor as she followed me. "Don't you want to see the rest of the building first?"

I shook my head and offered a single wave as I

headed back out to my town car. My breath low and heavy, it took everything I had to maintain my composure. After what we did the day before, she should've at least had the decency to tell me herself that she wasn't coming.

Angry, trembling fingers dialed her number, and just when I thought she was about to let it go to voicemail, she answered.

"Hi, Wilder." She spoke slowly, her words a timid, quiet whisper.

"You sent your assistant? Are you fucking kidding me?"

"Calm down. It's not that big of a deal. I got caught up at work."

"You couldn't have told me yourself?"

"Something came up last minute and I didn't think it'd be that big of a deal."

"Bull-fucking-shit, Addison. You knew exactly what you were doing." I raked my hand down across my face, pulling hard on the skin of my cheeks until it bounced back. I was sure I'd left marks, but I didn't care. "By the way, your assistant is a terrible liar. And you should tell her it's not professional to throw herself at your clients."

"I hope you were nicer to her than you're being to me." Her words were quick and almost entitled, as if I owed it to be cordial after the fucking hack job she'd done on my heart.

"God, Addison," I growled. "I was fucking balls deep in that uptight pussy of yours yesterday. The least you can do is be honest with me and not avoid me like some kind of coward."

Her end of the phone was silent a little too long, though I heard her draw in a long, slow breath. "You want honesty? Fine. I need space."

"Space?! Space from what? Yesterday was the first time I'd seen you in two weeks."

"I need even more space so I can fall out of love with you."

Her action that afternoon was like a knife to my heart, and her words were the final twist.

So that was it. She loved me, and she didn't want to love me anymore. I couldn't keep fighting a losing battle.

"You want space?" I seethed. "Fine. See you at Christmas, sis."

I hung up on her. It wasn't a classy move, but an angry Wilder was far from a classy Wilder.

My phone vibrated in my hand, and for a split second I hoped maybe it was her, calling to say she took it all back. That she didn't give a fuck about what anyone else thought. She wanted to be with me.

Instead, it was my father.

Groaning, I debated letting it go to voicemail, but then again, I didn't want to miss *the phone call.* The one I always got after he'd been with a woman for an indeterminate amount of time. The one where he called to say he was leaving her and things weren't working out the way he'd hoped.

"Hey, Dad," I said, my voice probably a little too chipper.

"Wilder, hi! You answered." He seemed pleasantly surprised to hear my voice, and he sure as hell didn't sound like a man who was ending a marriage so fresh the ink wasn't even dry on the paperwork yet. "How you doing, son? Haven't heard from you since we left town a couple weeks ago. How's life?"

I didn't want to talk about it. Not with him. "Things are fine. What's up?"

"Just calling to see if you're coming on vacation with the family in a couple weeks."

Shit. I'd completely forgotten. He'd casually mentioned it that day we spent together, but my mind was so focused on other things I'd neglected to give it much thought beyond that.

"Oh," I said, searching for a believable excuse. "Two weeks? Um…"

"You said it shouldn't be a problem," he said. "That's what you told me. I booked us a five-bedroom house right on the beach. One of those timeshares I wanted you to invest in with me."

That's what it was all about. He didn't give two shits about family time. He wanted to get me to see the timeshares, like that'd be the final nail in the coffin of the shady deal he wanted to finalize with me. I had no intentions of agreeing to let him take two million dollars of my hard earned money and plug some leaking ship with it, but I'd have to figure out a way to tell him that another time.

"Are the girls going?" I asked.

"They sure are. Tammy Lynn just booked their flights this morning. I'm looking at their itineraries right now. I just need to know if you're going, son. I can put it on my credit card for Sky Miles and then write it off for work since we're looking at properties."

Addison's words played in my head. She asked for space. She didn't want to see me. Showing up in Florida would upset her, and as fucking pissed as I was about the whole thing, I wasn't that big of an asshole.

"Aw, don't make me beg," my dad laughed. "I really want you to come. Tammy Lynn's so excited. She's got all these big family dinners planned. We'll be right on the ocean. There's a beautiful, private beach just a short walk away. The house we're staying in has been renovated and each bedroom has a suite."

He sounded like such a salesman.

"Let me get back to you on that," I said. "I have to take a look at my schedule. I'll let you know soon."

"Plane tickets get more expensive the closer you get to the dates," my dad said. Sometimes he still spoke to me as if I were a broke college student and not an independently wealthy man. "You know that. Anyway, just let me know."

"I can get my own ticket, Dad. That is, if I go. Again, I'll let you know."

nineteen

addison

"Addison, sweetie, what's the matter?"

Wilder had just hung up on me when Brenda Bliss walked by and happened to see me dabbing my eyes with a tissue. She rushed toward me, suddenly all motherly, and slipped her arm around my back.

"I don't know what's going on with you, but lately you've been off your game."

Her words stung, but they were true. I couldn't argue with that. I used to be a shark. I used to be relentless and constantly "on" as I raked in sale after sale and nonstop networked. Now I was nothing but a floating jellyfish, emotions transparent and set to casually sting anyone who dared come near me.

"I'm sorry, Brenda." I inhaled sharply and focused on the sensation of cool air renewing my lungs. "I'm just dealing with some… family things… I shouldn't let them affect my work, but I guess I am."

"Why don't you get out of here? Take the rest of the day. Shoot, take the rest of the week. Go do something for you," she suggested. Brenda Bliss practically lived at the office. It was rare she told anyone to take time off, especially considering time off in the real estate world was unpaid. If we weren't working, we weren't getting sales and Brenda Bliss Agency was losing money. "I want you to come back here Monday completely recharged. I want to see the girl I hired. The girl that's going to take over Manhattan real estate someday soon…"

She offered me a kind wink and cordial smile before slipping away and leaving my office. I shut my laptop and locked my desk before gathering my things and heading home.

"Hey, Coco." I called my sister as I walked home, taking a sharp turn at the halfway mark and heading back uptown. Everything about me felt deflated, and I was certain she could hear it in my voice. "Can I come over?"

"Of course," she said. "I just got home from hot yoga, but I'm here. I need to hop in the shower, but you can just come over."

By the time I arrived, the kettle on the stove was whistling and Coco was simultaneously flitting around the kitchen pulling ceramic mugs from the cabinet and drying her hair with a microfiber towel.

"I have some of that lemongrass green tea you like." She poured some steaming water into my cup and unwrapped a tea bag.

"Thanks, Co."

"What's on your mind?" Her blue eyes searched mine. "Wait. I think I know."

I expected her to roll her eyes. To tell me to toughen up. Insist I'd done the right thing and the pain would go away soon. Instead she climbed up onto the bar stool next to me and laid her wet, soggy head against my shoulder.

"You're not you anymore," she said. "Ever since you ended it with that guy. With our new stepbrother." She placed air quotes around the word I'd grown to hate. "I miss you. The girl you were when you were with him. You were happier then. You're not happy anymore."

I tilted my head, my cheek hitting the top of her wet hair. "I miss him so much, Co."

"Are you still working with him? Selling him properties?"

"Technically, yeah. I don't think I should anymore. You should see him now. He's not himself, either. It's like he's been replaced with this… darker version of himself. Like his heart's turned black or something. And it's all my fault."

"Psh," Coco said, sitting up. "You can thank Tammy Lynn for marrying some random guy who just happened to be Wilder's dad. She sure can pick 'em."

"I just can't get over how happy she is now. I've never seen her this way. She's suddenly the mom we always dreamed of having."

"It's not going to last. You know it's all an act. She's pretending like she gives two fucks about us because that's what Vince wants to see."

I lifted the steeped tea to my mouth, blowing first and then taking a careful sip. "You know, I could wait until this whole thing blows over and she divorces Vince, but who knows when that'll be? She was married to the last guy for three years. Three years from now, Wilder will have long moved on."

"Is he coming to Florida?" Coco changed the subject, sort of.

I set the teacup down, my heart racing. "I hadn't thought about it. I have no idea. I doubt it."

Coco ruffled the towel over her hair one last time and finger combed it into place. "Why's that?"

"I told him I needed space."

Her lips bunched in the corner as she drew in a deep breath. "I really hope Mom divorces Vince. I hate seeing you this sad. When you're sad, I'm sad. And I'm this close to telling you to just fucking be with the guy."

"But your career," I objected. If me being with Wilder had any adverse consequences for her career, I'd never forgive myself. As her sister, I couldn't do that to her. And if her career went tumbling down over some stepbrother-stepsister scandal, I'd be next. "I'm not going to put your future at jeopardy. I love you, Coco. I'm not doing that to you."

"I appreciate it," she said, a hint of her Kentucky twang emerging. She'd told me endless stories in the past about a certain subset of journalists and Susannah Jethro loyalists who'd do anything to get their hands on a single piece of dirt that would take her down. "Though it doesn't make me happy, I'll tell you that. Have you thought about talking to Mom about him? Maybe come clean and tell her why you were acting so weird at the restaurant? You never know. She might decide to put her daughter's happiness before hers, for once."

"She loves Vince. I can't ask her to not to be with him."

"She doesn't deserve you as a daughter." Coco raised her brows. "You're handling this a lot better than I would."

Wilder's words burned in my mind, *"You're a goddamned saint, Addison… that's your fucking problem."*

* * *

Two weeks later…

I'd emailed Wilder several listings, never getting a single response. I'd even sent him some referrals for new agents. Still nothing. I supposed it was his way of giving me space. I couldn't blame him. He was only doing exactly what I'd asked.

It didn't help that every tall, dark-haired man in a three-piece suit strolling the city sidewalks of Manhattan looked like him. I searched for him everywhere I went. Every restaurant. Every showing. Every open house.

He was never there, and it was as if I'd wished him away. Like he never existed in the first place.

"I don't know about you, but I'm ready for some sun." Coco stretched her pale arms in front of her as we settled into our spots on the plane. "It's been such a cold, gray spring."

"I got us a convertible rental car," I said, nudging her arm. "A Mustang."

"Do you even remember how to drive?"

"Of course I do. It's like riding a bike."

"Not really."

"How hard can it be?"

"You haven't owned a car in, like, eight years. Do

you still have a license?"

"Of course I do. And I promise I'll get us where we need to go, all right? Just trust me." I shoved my purse beneath the seat in front of me and pulled out a tabloid magazine I'd picked up in the gift shop. Flipping through, I stopped when a spread in the middle caught my eye.

It was an article about Coco's ex-boyfriend, Beau, and how he was permanently retiring from the music business for personal reasons. The article quoted many close sources to him, stating he was refusing to give an official interview. I felt her eyes over my shoulder as she pretended not to read it.

"You want this when I'm done? You can maybe cut out his picture. Frame it. Kiss it goodnight…"

Coco huffed and rolled her eyes. "Who gives a shit about him? I don't know what the big deal is anyway. He's not that great."

They were all lies she told herself to sandbag the gaping hole he'd left in her heart since they'd parted ways after high school. Being the good sister I was, I closed the tabloid and tucked it into the seat pocket in front of me. I'd have to read it later. "I agree, Co. I don't see what all the fuss is about."

"Can I offer you some champagne?" the flight attendant interrupted us with a grand commercial smile across her pretty face. Mom and Vince had paid for our tickets, but we'd paid to upgrade to First Class when we checked in. Coco tended to be left alone when she flew First Class, and I wasn't going to turn down the extra legroom.

Four hours later, we were cruising down I-95 with the top down on the convertible as the wind whipped our hair. Well, at least it whipped my hair. Coco decided to go all Jackie Kennedy and wrapped a silk scarf around her dark locks. We found the beach house shortly after arriving in Cocoa Beach and parked the car in the circle drive.

"They really went all out," I said as we tugged our overloaded suitcases out of the trunk of the Mustang. The white beach house with the wraparound porch and sundeck had to have cost a small fortune to rent, though I presumed it all came out of Vince's pocket. He seemed like a man who liked to toss around the fact that he may or may not be rolling in the dough. It was a real estate agent thing. Some agents had to project an image of wealth and enormous success to land the larger contracts. I supposed Vince felt the need to project that image 24/7, because he sure as hell didn't need to impress us.

"Hello, hello," Coco called as we showed ourselves in. Gauzy curtains flanking open sliders toward the back of the house led us to a covered porch where Mom and Vince were enjoying margaritas with salted rims. The inside of the house was slightly dated with decorative schemes ranging from sea foam green to shades of peach I never knew existed, but in a nostalgic vacation sort of way, that didn't bother me in the slightest. People didn't stay there for the seashell and nautical-themed rooms. They stayed for the ocean view.

"They're here!" Mom stood up and practically ran to us, wrapping us in hugs and refusing to take the ridiculous smile off her face.

Vince stood up, one hand in his pocket while the other gripped his frozen drink, and waved a friendly hello, which was appreciated since we weren't exactly on hugging terms yet.

"Have a seat, girls," Mom said as she strutted toward the kitchen. "I'll pour you some drinks. We have a margarita machine!"

The salty ocean breeze ruffled my hair and the warm, thick air was like a calming embrace. I needed that. I needed to get away from the city and Wilder and work. We were there for five days, and I fully intended on planting my toes in the sand and not moving a single muscle all week.

"Wilder should be here soon," Vince said as he sat back down and took a sip of his drink.

"W-what did you say?" I stammered. His words knocked the wind right out of my sails. I glanced over at Coco who raised her eyebrows like she didn't know a damn thing about it, either. My cheeks burned hot and my hands clammed up I gulped in humid air. "I didn't think he was coming?"

Maybe it wasn't that I didn't know he was coming. I just *assumed* he wasn't coming. I'd asked him to give me space and he'd listened. Coming to Florida to spend a week in a house with me would defeat the whole purpose of him avoiding me the last two weeks.

And while I was convinced space was what I needed to make me fall out of love with him, the reaction coursing through my body at Vince's mere mention of Wilder coming told me I was far from over him. I wasn't even close.

"Here we are, girls." My mom sat two overfilled

margaritas in front of us, and I practically lunged for the thing. "How was your flight?"

"It was fine," Coco said, spinning her glass between her thumb and pointer finger. Ever since she saw that article about Beau, she'd kept getting lost in thought. Every time I looked at her, she had some faraway look on her face.

A rustling coming from the inside of the house drew my attention toward the open sliding door behind me. Shuffling footsteps and the sound of luggage being hauled were enough to tell me the guest of honor had arrived. I couldn't think straight. I hadn't planned to see him.

"Wilder, my boy!" Vince stood up and headed into the house. "I'm so glad you decided to come!"

Oh, so he wasn't going to come?

I turned to face him and offered him a dismal smile. We were going to have to make the best of things that week. "Hi, Wilder. How are you?"

"Hey, sis!" His tone was sarcastic, though I was quite certain I was the only one who picked up on that. He leaned down and wrapped his arms around me, squeezing me tight and forcing me to breathe in the intoxicating scent of his aftershave. The one that had felt like home just weeks ago.

"You want a drink? Here, have a seat." Vince offered Wilder his chair, which happened to be right across from me, as he headed inside. Emerging with a beer a minute later, he handed it to Wilder.

"Thanks, Dad," Wilder said with a Wally Cleaver smile as he pulled the tab on the beer can and took a drink. His eyes held mine prisoner, refusing to let go.

I mouthed the word "what" and scrunched my nose at him. What was he trying to do here?

"Well, since everyone's here, I better get supper started." My mom sprung to action and headed inside, humming a quiet, happy tune.

"If you don't mind, I feel like taking a walk on the beach before we eat," Wilder said, still looking directly at me. He scooted out from the table and headed down the deck and toward the path that led straight to the sandy beach.

"What's that about?" Coco turned to me, and I shrugged.

"No clue," I said.

"We brought some card games," Vince said. He hadn't removed the cheesy T.V. dad grin from his face since we'd arrived. "Thought maybe after dinner the five of us could sit out here and have some good, old-fashioned family fun?"

"Aw, family time," Coco whispered just loud enough that I could hear her. I jabbed my elbow into her side when Vince turned away.

My gaze was still on Wilder, watching as he slowly trudged through the sand in his bare feet, his shoes in one hand and his beer in the other. He wore a pair of faded red shorts and an untucked, wrinkled baby blue button down. I'd never seen him dressed down before. He was always in a suit and tie, or at the very least a polo or cashmere sweater. His hair was a product-free mess, and judging by his little episode a second earlier, he was definitely not himself.

It was safe to say that Wilder Van Cleef had come undone.

twenty

addison

"Aw, reverse! Back to *Addi*," Wilder exclaimed during a game of *Uno* later that night. A fresh, frosty beer rested in his hand as he slapped a yellow reverse card down in the center pile. He'd insisted on sitting next to me when the game started, and he continued to reverse the order so he could strategically pick on me. Every time he'd pick a color he knew I didn't have, he'd nudge me with his elbow or lean into me for a brief moment. "I don't know about you guys, but I think I kind of love being a big brother."

Coco and I exchanged looks before I said, "You certainly seem to be wearing the title well."

He reached his arm around my shoulder, pulling me into him. "My whole life, all I wanted was a little sister. And now I finally got one. Two, actually."

"Lucky you," I mumbled.

Mom flashed a rosy-cheeked, happy-in-love look Vince's way as he placed his hand over hers.

If they only knew…

"So, Wilder," Vince said. "You're turning the big two-eight tomorrow. Tammy Lynn would love to bake you a cake."

She never baked us birthday cakes growing up.

"Aw, that's too sweet of you, Tammy Lynn. You don't have to do that for me." He drew a card and jabbed an elbow into my side to tell me it was my turn.

"Oh, please. I want to. It means so much to me that you came out here to join us," she said. "When Vince said you might not come, I was worried that maybe you didn't want to accept us as your family. I'm glad you changed your mind."

"So, buddy, you thinking about settling down anytime soon?" Vince took a sip of his drink as he slapped a red number three down and then reorganized the remaining cards in his hand. "You're not getting any younger! When I was your age, I had *you* already."

"You know, the girls have so many friends and connections in the city," Mom gushed. "I'm sure they could introduce you to a nice, young woman."

"Thank you, no." Wilder said, turning my way. "My heart already belongs to someone."

"You didn't tell me you were dating anyone!" Vince leaned across the table and pounded his fist into Wilder's shoulder. "You old dog, you. Tell us about her."

My heart thudded hard in my chest, and the margarita from earlier sloshed around in my stomach as it threatened to rise up into my mouth. Had he moved on already? So soon?

"Let's see…" Wilder leaned back in his seat as the corners of his lips curled upward. "She's a little bit younger than me, but that's okay because she acts way older."

My eyes widened. I listened intently as I stared down at my hand of cards. My mind immediately pictured someone like Skylar: young, huge breasts, and beautiful. Wilder could easily get any girl he wanted just by snapping his fingers.

"I'll spare you the details," he said, his jaw hardening and his posture suddenly stiff. Wilder's annoying big brother façade was fading fast. "She's special. That's all I'll say. I knew it from the moment we met."

Lightheadedness flooded me as my lungs gasped for air. I needed to go lie down. Imagining him with another woman, real or not, was too much to take.

"So, you think you met the one?" Vince asked, all smiles.

"Oh, I don't think. I know." Wilder slammed a card down in the stack and then nudged me. "Your turn, *sis*."

"What are you waiting for, son? When do you think you'll ask her?" Vince leaned forward, anxiously awaiting his answer. I supposed that to people of our parents' generation, people who married young and sometimes repeatedly, the fact that Wilder was an unmarried twenty-eight year old was concerning.

"Never." Wilder placed his hand of cards face down on the table and finished the last of his beer before turning to look directly at me. "She doesn't love me."

I practically choked on my spit. My hand flew to my mouth as I tried to control the coughing fit that followed. He'd been talking about me the entire time.

"What?" Vince scrunched his brows together. "Now that's just ridiculous. How could anyone not love you back?"

"I don't know, Dad," Wilder said as he looked at me. "I wish I could ask her, but she's a little closed off."

Mom wiped her eye and offered a bittersweet smile. "I really hope you meet someone special someday, Wilder. Maybe you'll forget all about this girl. She doesn't deserve you anyway."

I tossed back the rest of my margarita and blinked away my watering eyes. I adjusted my body toward Coco and away from Wilder. I wasn't sure how much more I could take.

"I guess I'm just not what she wants. Nothing I can do about that." Wilder stood up and went to the kitchen, presumably to grab another drink, only he came back with a bottle of water. Even in his drunken stupor, he realized he needed to cool it.

"Maybe someday she'll come around," Mom said when he returned.

"And when she does, I'll be waiting," he said, his words toneless. He uncapped his water and took a sip. "Because that's what you do when you love somebody. You wait for them, no matter how hard it might be."

"Well, don't wait too long, son," Vince laughed. "There are plenty of fish in the sea. Cast your net wide and you'll find someone. Maybe you'll find someone you'll love even more. Sounds like she's maybe not worth the trouble."

"Can you all excuse me, please?" I slid out from the table and headed inside, grabbing my suitcase from the foyer and heading upstairs to an empty guest room. I couldn't take any more. I couldn't sit there and listen to him profess his love for me.

I loved the hell out of him. I just couldn't be with him. It was never that he wasn't what I wanted.

He was everything I wanted.

twenty-one

WILDER

We played another round of *Uno*, though my mind wasn't in the game. The empty seat next to me and the tepid ocean breeze that replaced it served to remind me that maybe I'd gone too far.

But she needed to hear what I had to say, and if that was the only way then so be it. I never expected her to run upstairs to get away from me, and I was almost certain I'd seen her crying.

"Uno!" Coco yelled, holding up her last remaining card. One more go-around and she laid down her final card, a blue seven. "Okay, I'm sitting this next one out."

"Actually, I think I've had enough games for tonight," I said. "I'm out, too."

I stood up. I needed to go find her somewhere in that big, white house.

"I think Vince and I are going to go for a little late night stroll on the beach," Tammy Lynn said, grabbing his hand. "It's too perfect of a night not to."

Coco stood to leave. "I need to get some work done on my laptop. I'll be in the family room if anyone needs me, I guess."

I waited for everyone to go their own way before heading inside and climbing the stairs. There were five bedrooms in that house, and I wasn't sure where she was hiding, but I sure as hell was going to find her.

The first door I knocked on went unanswered, so I swung it open. Nothing but a small empty room with pastel peach walls and a blue bedspread covered in faded seashells.

The second door I knocked on also went unanswered, but when I barged in, I was met with half-open suitcases probably belonging to Dad and Tammy Lynn.

I knocked on the third door, the one at the end of the east hallway.

"Go away," Addison sobbed.

Ding, ding, ding.

I ignored her plea and let myself in, closing the door behind me and heading to where she was curled up into a ball with her face buried in the ugliest, salmon-colored quilt I'd ever seen. Transparent curtains fluttered as the salty ocean breeze traveled in through the open windows.

We should've been laughing and talking and having a good time. We should've been trying to forge some kind of friendship. I should've been nicer to her, and maybe I shouldn't have shown up in the first place.

"Look, I'm sorry," I said, slowly crouching down to where she lay. She cried softly into the pillow. "I shouldn't have said what I said down there. At least, not in the way I said it."

She peered over her shoulder, her blue eyes wet

with runny black mascara.

"I meant every word, though." I climbed onto the bed, lying next to her and grabbing her thigh to hoist it over my hip. With my hand on the small of her back, I pulled her tight against me.

"You act," she sniffled, "like I don't want to be… with you… but you know that's not… it's not like that…"

I ran my hand over the back of her head, soothing her as she cried into my chest.

"W-why'd you come here?" she asked.

"Fuck, I don't know. I thought maybe if you saw me again, you'd remember how much you loved me. I'm a desperate man, lovely. A fucked up, desperate man, and this was my final act of desperation."

"Like I could possibly forget that I love you," she whimpered. "I never stopped, Wilder. Not once."

Without thinking, I leaned down and kissed away her salty tears. With my lips against her warm, soft cheeks, she pulled her face up. Staring into my soul with glassy eyes, she kissed me.

"One last time," she whispered as she sat up and climbed on top of me. Our fingers interlaced. "I miss the way you used to look at me."

I stared into the eyes of a girl whose world was spinning madly out of control, and she knew I was the only one who could fix it. My hands searched through the dark room until they found her face. Half her face glowed against the pale moonlight pouring in through the open windows. With her fingers tugging the hem of her top, she pulled it up and over her head before leaning down and kissing me again. The second her body was pressed against mine, I rolled her over, pinning her beneath me.

She used to love when I controlled her body. When I told her what to do. When she gave herself to me, she said she'd never felt more alive. My hand slipped down between us as I unbuttoned her jeans and tugged them off her hips.

I climbed off the bed. "Take everything off. Now."

She stifled a relieved smile as she willingly obliged, unhooking her bra and slipping her black lace panties down her shapely legs and kicking them to the floor.

"Lay on your stomach," I commanded. She rolled over, burying the side of her face in the pillow she'd previously cried into. My hands twitched as I undressed myself, one tedious button at a time. Pulling a condom from my wallet, I slid it over my hardened shaft and climbed back on the bed. I slid my hands underneath her hips until they reached her pussy. I slipped a finger inside with ease, aided by her overabundance of wetness. "God, you must really want this."

She nodded, biting her lip. "I do. So bad."

"Don't talk." I bent to the floor, grabbing my leather belt. I hooked it around the wrought iron headboard and wrapped it around her wrists. I'd have much preferred to make love to her in that bed and not fuck her, but I was simply following her orders. Next I grabbed her black panties and bunched them into a wad before gently placing them into her mouth. My right hand traveled back to her sweet pussy, pleasantly surprised to find it was even wetter than before.

I gathered her hair into a ponytail at her nape, tugging it back as I whispered in her ear. "We have to be quiet. Don't make a sound."

She nodded as soon as I released her hair. My hands lightly traced down her naked back, stopping at her round ass and grabbing a handful before pulling her hips up and forcing her into a kneeling position. I smoothed my hand across her ass before offering a quick slap that surely left an imprint.

"Mm," she said as the sting of the slap left her soft skin.

"Quiet, Addison," I growled. "You don't want me to do that again, do you?"

I slipped a finger inside her arousal once again, finding her more relaxed than usual, as if she'd wanted me more than she'd ever wanted me before. With my hand gripping the base of my cock, I guided it inside her slowly, one tantalizing inch at a time.

Her hips bucked back against mine in response to the deep insertion. Gripping her hips, I thrust in and out of her, slowly and then building in intensity. My hands crawled the length of her body, tracing every curve and angle, feeling what was mine. Claiming every inch of her.

The way she moved told me she wanted more, and she knew she wasn't allowed to speak. I had to listen to what she wasn't saying. I fucked her harder, harder than I'd ever fucked her before, she fucked me back, circling her hips and arching her spine when my fingers played against her swollen clit.

Her round breasts bounced with each thrust, and faint, uncontrollable sighs leaving her muffled mouth told me she was getting close. I slowed down. I wanted to enjoy it, and I sure as fuck wanted her to enjoy it, too.

I pulled myself out of her, knowing it was a tortuous act but one that would soon pay off. With her ass in the air and her face buried in the pillow on top of her restrained wrists, I positioned myself for reentry.

"Mm!" she moaned as her body accepted mine once more. I slapped her ass with each thrust before giving her respite. The way she fucked me back told me she was holding on to the earthquake rumbling in her core and never letting go. Hunched over her and gripping her hips, I jackhammered her swollen, pink pussy until she came all over my cock and I unleashed a stream of pent up frustration inside her.

I collapsed on top of her, our bodies sweaty from the humid Florida air seeping in the open window. We stuck together like Velcro as I tugged the panties from her pretty much and unwrapped the leather belt from her wrists.

I slinked off her and laid flat on the opposite side of the bed, attempting to catch my breath. And when I very least expected it, she curled up into my arm. The way she used to.

"What's this?" I whispered.

She nuzzled against my chest, placing an open palm on my stomach.

"I'm going to leave tomorrow," I said, keeping my voice low. I wasn't sure how much time had passed, but I knew it was late. For all I knew the walls of the beach house were paper thin and there were three unsuspecting souls who would ruin this moment for us if they only knew what we'd just done.

"Why?"

"I can't be around you like this and not want to keep touching you. And I can't pretend. I thought I could, but I can't."

"You don't have to go…" Her voice trailed as she tugged me tight. "Shit. You're right. They're going to know something's up if you keep sneaking into my room like this."

"Sounds like someone didn't fall out of love with me like she planned," I teased, dragging the tips of my fingers against her arm.

"Not at all," she giggled. "Did you mean it when you said you'd wait for me?"

"I did." I drew in a sharp breath. "I don't think I have a choice. The heart wants what it wants. I'm never going to meet another girl who makes me feel half the things you make me feel."

I rolled to my side, pressing her onto her back. Even with dried streaks of mascara around her pretty blue eyes, she was still beautiful.

"You forget I'm an investor," I whispered, lowering my lips to the crevice between her breasts. "I'm a very patient man, Addison. I can wait a long time if it means getting what I want."

She smiled as I gathered her arms and placed them above her head. I crawled over top of her, pinning her once more. I just wanted to feel the warmth of our naked bodies as the night air clung to our skin.

I kissed her left breast, just above her pert, pink nipple. "That's an investment." My lips traveled to her collarbone. "That's another investment." I kissed the tender underside of her neck. "And another investment…"

She laughed, melting away the day's tension. "What the hell are you talking about?"

"One day these investments are going to mature,"

I explained. "And I'll cash out."

"Cash out?"

"Yeah, cash out. Marry you."

Her hand flew to my face, cupping my jaw as she stared at me exactly the way she did when we first realized we had absolutely no control over what was happening between us.

"Funny way of putting it, but I think I get it," she said with a laugh.

"It's good seeing you again," I said. "The real you. Not the crazy you."

"Same here. I was worried about you for a little bit. You get kind of scary when…"

"When the things I love have been ripped away from me? Yeah. It goes way back. I'm sorry." I pulled her close, kissing her soft lips again and reveling in their sweet taste.

"What are we going to do until our parents' divorce?" she asked, her face suddenly falling.

"Let's not worry about that." I stroked the side of her cheek. "Let's just enjoy this. Right here. Right now."

She lay in my arms all night, and we talked until

two or three in the morning, keeping our voices low. At some point I must have fallen asleep in her bed, because the next thing I knew someone was knocking at her door.

"Addison?"

I popped up. "Shit, Addison. Your mom's out there."

"Fuck," she said, springing to action. We both glanced down at the floor where our clothes were strewn. "Get in the closet."

I flew to the closet, sliding one of the mirrored doors aside and stepping in, pulling it shut slowly and quietly.

"Addison, are you awake?"

"Hold on, Mom. Coming," I heard her yell back. A minute later, her mom's voice grew closer, as if she were seated on Addison's bed.

"It's nine o'clock. Aren't you going to get up? I think Coco talked about going for a jog on the beach. It'd be nice of you to join her."

"I will," she said.

"Have you seen Wilder?" I heard Tammy Lynn ask. "He wasn't in his room this morning."

Shit.

"Um, no, I went to bed last night after the game. I haven't seen him. Sorry."

"Mmhm."

"What?"

"It's just that every time you're around him, you just act so strange. I can't put my finger on it, but I have noticed it. I don't know him well enough yet to know if he's always so smart-mouthed, or if he's pulling out all the stops for us."

I stifled a laugh.

"You sure nothin's wrong, baby?" Tammy Lynn asked once again. "You know you can tell me anything."

Come on, Addison. Tell her. Now's your chance.

"I'm sure, Mom. Everything's fine."

"What do you think of Vince, sweetie?" Tammy Lynn asked, her tone suddenly chipper. "You like him so far?"

"Yeah. I mean, he seems to make you happy."

"You think we're a good match? He's just so different from my usual type."

"He's not covered in leather and tattoos and he doesn't drive a motorcycle, but I think it's safe to say he's a step up. Why? Are you having doubts?"

"No, no," Tammy Lynn insisted. "I was just curious as to what you thought."

Silence filled the space between them for a little too long before the sound of shuffling feet moved toward the door.

"Get washed up, sweetie, and come down for breakfast. Hopefully Wilder shows up around here somewhere."

"Maybe he passed out on the beach. He seemed kind of drunk last night," Addison said.

"Who knows?"

The click of the door shutting brought Addison over to the closet. "Oh, my God. That was close."

"You should've told her."

"What are you talking about?"

"About us. She asked if you were okay. You should've been honest."

Addison's shoulders fell as she clasped her hands across her heart. "She's so happy. I can't ruin that for her.

I'm sorry. It doesn't change how I feel about you. Nothing could change that."

The euphoric high from the night spent holding her in my arms evaporated into thin, sea salted air. I didn't have a right to be mad at her. She hadn't made any promises, and I'd hushed her when she tried talking about the future.

"Don't be mad." Her blue eyes pled with mine as she reached for me, placing a warm palm on my crossed arms. She drew near and leaned up on her toes, planting a soft kiss on my lips. "Please don't go home today. You're here. Just stay. Let's make the best of it. We'll figure things out when we get back home."

twenty-two

addison

A week had passed since we all returned from Florida. I'd yet to show Wilder a property, but I'd seen him once in passing on the street. I was headed back to the office from a client meeting and bumped into him, so we stopped into a little coffee shop and got a warm beverage and had a friendly chat.

After our week together at the beach house, we both agreed we had to keep each other at arm's length. No more secret sex sessions. No more stolen glances. We promised one another to keep things professional, no matter how much it hurt. And we promised not to see other people, which was extremely easy on my part since I didn't have time to date anyway.

I slid into my leather office chair on a balmy May morning and checked my email, smiling when I saw one from Wilder declaring he wanted to make an offer on one of the warehouses I'd shown him a few weeks back. Having him for a client meant I could scale back a bit on my workload and still come out on top professionally, which was wonderful. I'd been burning the candle at both ends for as long as I could remember.

Kyle seemed to be losing clients left and right, and I wasn't sure whether or not Brenda Bliss had a hand in it or if somehow Wilder was working a little behind-the-scenes magic. He knew a lot of people in the industry and was one of the most well-connected investors I'd ever come across, though he never acted like it. I neglected to ask Wilder about it, not wanting to know the truth. Though if he did have something to do with the gradual demise of Kyle's career, he probably wouldn't admit to it anyway.

My phone buzzed on the table. Mom was calling.

"Hey, Mom, what's up? I'm at the office," I answered.

She sighed, long and heavy, into the phone. It was never a good thing when she did that. I'd heard that sigh before. Several times, actually. "I'm leaving Vince."

I thanked God that she couldn't see the enormous grin forming across my face in that moment. "Oh, no, Mom. Why? What happened?"

"I'm just miserable with him, sweetie." She sounded like a deflated balloon, and the nasally sound of her voice suggested she was lying down on the sofa at home. I could just picture her with her left arm draped across her forehead as if she were sick.

"You two seemed so happy, though. In New York and at the beach. I'd never seen you like that before." I scratched my head. Nothing was adding up.

"He's a nice man, Addison, don't get me wrong. He just bores me to tears with how everything has to be so perfect all the time. Perfect wife. Perfect little life. Perfect family. If he buys me another twinset from J.C. Penney, I think I'm going to die."

"But I thought that was what you wanted? A perfect nuclear family kind of life?"

"I thought maybe that would make me happy. It didn't. I was still just as miserable as I was before. I never should've married him," she groaned. "When am I going to learn, huh? I'm fifty-three years old."

"Fifty-eight."

"Fine. I'm fifty-eight years old, and I've got four failed marriages under my belt."

"Five."

"Five, whatever. I'm so embarrassed." I heard her sniffle, though it seemed like her hand had covered the receiver for a brief second. "God, he's a horrible kisser. He doesn't have a single tattoo anywhere on him. He goes to bed at nine o'clock every night. I'm surprised he doesn't suggest we have separate beds, for Christ's sakes."

Funny how Wilder could come from a man like that. "I had no idea he was that vanilla, Mom."

"Well, lesson learned," she said. "I think I need to be single for a while."

She'd said that very phrase a million times before. It'd lost its meaning years ago. "Yeah, maybe you should be single for a while."

"Besides," she sighed, "Dakota told me everything."

"Excuse me?"

"I know all about you and Wilder."

My heart raced and my response lodged itself in my throat.

"It explains a lot," she laughed. "I mean, the behavior, you two running off together at the restaurant. The Uno debacle. I guess I was too blind to see it. Dakota filled in all the blanks for me."

"She always did have a big mouth," I mused, secretly thankful.

"Anyway, I had a long talk with your sister about everything the other day, and it just sort of finalized my decision to leave Vince. I'm not happy with him, and you want to be with Wilder. It's a no-brainer, sweetie. You have no idea what it means to know that you were going to put your happiness on hold for me. You're a good daughter, and I don't deserve you."

"You're leaving Vince for sure?" I asked. With my brain suspended in a state of shock and disbelief, I could hardly process the life changing magnitude of our conversation. Something about me being a good daughter. Perhaps I should've focused on the kind words she was sharing, and any other day her words would've gone down in history. Tammy Lynn never paid compliments, not ones that exposed her innermost feelings.

"For sure," she said.

"You're not going to change your mind?"

"Never. My mind's made up."

"Mom?" Hot tears fogged my vision as I let them pool and fall onto the desktop below me.

"Yes, baby?" she drawled.

"Thank you." I hung up with her and immediately dialed Coco. "I can't believe you!"

"What?" Coco drew the word out, and I could only imagine the mischievous look on her face.

"Mom just called me. Said you told her everything about Wilder and me." I wanted to hug her, but making her squirm a little was more fun.

"Yeah?" Coco said. "I did."

"Why?"

"I did it because you're my sister and I love you more than words, and I want you to be happy," she said. "You deserve to be happy, Addison. You should be with Wilder."

"Have I told you how much I love you lately?" My mind whirred and whizzed in fifty different ecstatic directions. The second I had a chance, I was going to find Wilder, wherever the hell he was, and jump into his arms. "Did Mom tell you she was leaving Vince?"

"She mentioned it, yes. But she wanted to be the one to tell you, so I didn't say anything. You know, after everything Mom put us through when we were younger, I figured it was her turn to make a sacrifice so that one of us could be happy."

"That's one way to look at it."

"I knew you were too nice to say anything, so I had to intervene. I couldn't stand her prancing around like Betty Crocker on Vince's arm while you were crying yourself to sleep every night."

"Thanks, Co. I mean it. Thank you."

"Just doing my job," she laughed. "That's what big sisters are for, right? To get in everyone's business and right the wrongs."

"You're the glue, you know that? You've always been the glue in our little family."

"All right, enough of this sentimental bullshit. Hang up with me so you can go find him." Coco couldn't help being bossy. It was just the way she was made.

* * *

"Call me as *soon* as you get this." I left a quick voicemail on Wilder's phone. He didn't answer when I called. I drummed my fingers against my desk. I was as good as useless the rest of the day.

I gathered my things and told Skylar I was headed out to meet a client, though really I was headed to Wilder's office. I'd only been there once before, when we first started seeing each other. He had to stop by and grab a document, but it was after hours and we decided to get frisky on his desk, only to be interrupted by the cleaning lady.

I smiled as my heels pounded the pavement toward his work.

"I'm here to see Wilder Van Cleef," I said to his assistant when I checked in a short while later.

"He's on a conference call right now," she said, clicking around on her computer screen. "It looks like he'll be free in an hour. You can wait here, if you'd like?"

"This is extremely urgent," I said with a kind smile. "Can I just go in? I won't interrupt his call. I just need to—I need to see him."

"I'm very sorry. I can't let you go in there," she said.

"I'm his girlfriend," I said.

Her lips curled into a smile. "Mr. Van Cleef doesn't date. Nice try."

I drew in a sharp breath, telling myself she was just doing her job. "I promise you will not get in trouble if you just let me go in there."

"Mr. Van Cleef is very particular about—"

"Trust me, honey, I know how particular he can be." I didn't feel like standing around arguing with his pit bull any more. Clenching onto my purse, I turned on my heels and headed straight for his office.

"You can't go in there!" she yelled from her desk.

I barged into his office, where he was leaning back in his chair while a man on the other end droned on about beginning market values and a potential bidding war.

"Addison?" he mouthed. His brows met in the

middle and he cocked his head to the side.

I jumped up and down like a giddy school girl, flapping my hands and smiling like a damn idiot. I didn't care though. I was about to deliver the best news of my life to my favorite person in the whole world.

"Hey, Darryl, can I call you back in a bit?" Wilder interrupted him. "Something urgent came up that I need to deal with. Just give me a few minutes, okay?"

Darryl grunted into the phone. "I don't have all day, Wilder."

"I know, I know. Give me a few."

Wilder ended the call and replaced the receiver as I climbed into his lap and straddled him.

"You going to tell me what's going on?" he asked, slipping his hands around my waist.

I smirked. "It's happening. Vince and Tammy Lynn are divorcing."

"Are you kidding me?" He cupped my face and brought it toward his, pressing his lips hard onto mine. "So, what does this mean?"

"Everything, Wilder. It means everything."

He stood up, cupping my ass as he sat me on his

desk and pressed his hips into mine. “So, this is it? We can finally be together?”

“Mmhm.” I nuzzled into his neck, inhaling the clean scent of his aftershave as he buried his fingers into my golden waves.

He gently gathered my hair into his fist, guiding my head away from his neck until ours eyes met. “There’s something you should know about me right now.”

My eyes squinted as I silently prayed he wasn’t about to drop a bomb on me. Not now. Not when everything was going so well. “What’s that?”

“I’m never letting you go, no matter what.”

epilogue

addison

"Ladies and gentleman, may I have your attention please?" Brenda Bliss stood up at the podium in front of a gathering of thousands of Manhattan real estate agents. It was the annual end-of-year gala for the Manhattan Association of Listing Professionals; the time of year when the top ten agents in the city were announced. Brenda was the secretary of the association, but she loved to have all eyes on her, so she volunteered to emcee that year. At least that was what she'd told me when she made it clear my attendance was required.

The banquet hall silenced save for the rogue clinking of silver as attendees turned their focus to Brenda. Wilder reached beneath the tablecloth and grabbed my hand, squeezing it tight. I'd worked my ass off that year, making Wilder's investment company my main priority. I scoured the city and investigated leads and tips, finding him quick flips and a few great long-term ventures.

"Thank you all so much for being here with us tonight," Brenda said as microphone feedback stung our ears. "I know we all have a million and one engagements this time of year, and it's snowing pretty good outside. We'd all rather be cozied up in our *brownstones* and *condos* with a glass of brandy and a warm fire. Perhaps you'd rather be looking out from the windows of your *pied-a-terres* as the sparkling snow decorates the city we all hold dear."

The crowd erupted in polite laughter.

"But at the end of the day, we're all here for a reason. We love what we do, and we want to honor our best colleagues. Each year, only a select few can hold the coveted title of top one percent, and even a smaller few can be recognized as the top one percent of the top one percent. This year, I am pleased to announce that the top agent in all of Manhattan is one of my own."

Wilder squeezed my hand, and I glanced down at our interlocked fingers, the brilliant, cushion-cut stone on my left ring finger catching the dimmed light of the flickering candles that donned each tabletop around us.

"I've worked with this young woman since she started as my assistant a few short years ago. They always say the cream rises to the top, and ladies and gentleman, let me tell you, Addison Andrews is the crème-de-la-crème. Everyone, please give a warm welcome to the Manhattan Association of Listing Professionals' agent of the year, Addison Andrews!"

Wilder released my hand and rose to a standing position as I swept my long gown behind me and headed up to the podium to accept my award. I was convinced I wouldn't receive the award that year. There had been rumors of a few other agents sealing last-minute contracts that would blow my final numbers out of the water, but they must've fallen through.

"Wow," I said, clutching the polished gold in my sweaty palm. The small award, a gold depiction of a high-rise building, felt heavier than I imagined it would. "Thank you so much, everyone. I did not expect this."

The applause ceased and my eyes searched the dim room for my Wilder. He took his seat and leaned back, watching with a proud smile across his sexy lips.

"I'd like to thank Brenda Bliss, for taking me under her wing several years ago. She took a chance on me, and it means the world to me to make her proud right now."

I swallowed, my throat dry. It was the moment I'd worked so hard for. Why didn't it feel as amazing as I always imagined?

"I'd also like to thank my fiancé, Wilder Van Cleef, for always believing in me and never giving up on us, even when things got hard. I'd also like to thank my sister, Coco Bissett." I glanced over at our table where Coco was seated across on the other side of my chair. "I wouldn't be here if it weren't for her. We made a promise to each other when we were little, to always help each other achieve our dreams no matter how hard it might seem. I can say wholeheartedly, I would not be standing here today if it weren't for her support and everything she's done for me."

A man standing stage left motioned for me to wrap it up. I smiled, feeling like I was an actress at the Oscars or something. I supposed to many, this trivial little real estate gala was a farce. Meant nothing. But to me, to have reached the pinnacle of my career at such a young age and against all odds, it meant the world.

"Again, thank you." I held my trophy up in the air and gathered the silk organza fabric of my navy dress in my hand as I stepped down from the stage. I wanted to remember the sound of the applause for as long as I lived.

"Well done, *lovely*," Wilder said as I sat down. He leaned over and kissed my cheek. "I knew you could do it."

"Thanks," I said, nuzzling into his neck.

As Brenda Bliss stood at the podium doling out awards for the next half hour, I lost myself in Wilder's aquamarine eyes and the rest of the world faded away.

Shortly after dinner was served, a live band began playing Sinatra classics and patrons circled the room, socializing.

"Addison." Brenda rushed up to our table, giving me a warm hug. "I am so proud of you. You have no idea how hard it was for me to keep that a secret. I've known for a week!"

Wilder shot me a look and I nodded. I'd given her the news that morning.

"I'm so sorry to hear you're leaving me, but I can't

say that I blame you," Brenda said, referring to the bomb I'd dropped on her earlier that day. I was starting my own agency, which would be under the umbrella of Wilder's corporation after we married the following year.

We'd already set the date. May eleventh. Approximately a year to the date we found out we could officially be together again. I had five months to plan a wedding and get my company off the ground. Life was about to get all kinds of chaotic, but in the best of ways.

"I know you'll do well," Brenda said, rubbing my back. "And if you ever need help or want to talk, I'm always a phone call away. Just don't poach any of my agents!" She laughed, though I knew she meant business. I'd never poach from her. It wasn't my style, and the last thing I needed was a big, red target on the back of my brand new agency.

"You have nothing to worry about," I assured her. "I don't operate like that. You know that."

"Oh, honey, I know." She smiled, her eyes crinkling at the corners. "I just can't believe you're leaving me. I'm happy for you though. You deserve this."

Her gaze left mine and traveled to Wilder.

"I wish you nothing but the best," she said as she

disappeared into a crowd of chatty salespeople.

I made my rounds with Wilder at my side and checked my watch. “My feet are killing me.”

“I have a driver outside waiting.” He leaned into me, breathing me in. “If you want to go now, I promise I won’t put up a fight.”

“I feel like I should stay. This is my night.” I didn’t want to stay, though. I’d scaled Everest and reached the top, and I was tired. I wanted to go home.

He took my hand, lifting it to his mouth and kissing my palm. “We’ll do whatever you want. Tonight’s all about you.”

My heart warmed. He made every night feel like my night.

“Sometimes I look at you, and I still can’t believe you’re all mine,” he said as he leaned into me, his voice a low grumble against a noisy backdrop.

“Forever and always,” I replied. I closed my eyes and drank him in, wanting to forever remember what it felt like to anchor myself to solid ground after one of the most tumultuous years of my life.

* * *

"Where are we going?" I asked after we left the banquet. A yawn escaped my lips, and I ached to get out of my dress and into something softer. Wilder's town car seemed to be heading toward Midtown and not Soho.

"Wouldn't you like to know," he said, his face expressionless but his eyes shining against the city lights.

"I thought we were going home? You know I hate surprises." My breath hitched, and I tilted my head to the side as I attempted to read the street signs that passed.

He grabbed my wrist, pulling me up into his lap before cupping my face with his hands. "Lovely, it's okay to let go every once in a while. Or did you forget?"

The town car pulled up to the W Hotel; the place where it all began.

about the author

Winter Renshaw recently celebrated her third 29th birthday. By day, she wrangles kids and dogs, and by night, she wrangles words. She loves photography and peonies and lipstick and isn't a huge fan of rude people. Chips and salsa are her jam, and so is cruising down the highway with the windows down and the air blasting while 80s rock blasts from the speakers of her Mom-UV.

If Winter sounds like someone you just might want to be friends with, please add her at www.facebook.com/winterrenshawauthor

thank you!

Thank you, dear reader, for choosing *my* book. I sincerely hope you enjoyed it, and I hope you'll look for more from me in the near future!

I know we're all crazy busy, but if you had just a minute and wanted to leave a review on Amazon, I'm *pretty* sure you'd make my day. I read them all, and I appreciate the time you took out of your schedule to leave a comment!

Love you all – and *thank you, thank you, thank you* for making my dreams come true!

With a grateful heart,

Winter

PS – Page ahead for a preview of NEVER IS A PROMISE, which will focus on Addison's sister, Coco, and her ex-boyfriend (and unrequited love), Beau!

preview

This is an unedited excerpt from NEVER IS A PROMISE – *coming spring 2015!*

I wasn't her, and I hadn't been her since the day I left Kentucky.

"Name please?" the airline agent asked over the phone as I booked my flight home.

"Coco – sorry, I mean Dakota," I said, running my fingers over the plastic raised imprint of my name as it read on my credit card. "Last name is Bissett."

"Please read off the numbers on the front of your card, ma'am," she said.

I rattled them off one by one, speaking slowly as if it could possibly prolong the inevitable. I didn't want to go home. I fought long and hard with Harrison about it, but any fight with him was a losing battle.

I scribbled my confirmation number along with the flight details on thick cardstock with my monogram across the top; a "B" in the middle that stood for Bissett flanked by a "C" on the left for Coco and an "E" on the right for Elizabeth.

"You're doing the right thing, Coco." Harrison christened me with the nickname "Coco" when I landed my first news-anchoring job. At the time, it was nothing more than a nickname, but over the years it had morphed into a brand. Coco Bissett was officially a household name.

Harrison slipped his hands over my shoulders and rubbed the kinks out as if he were still my doting husband. We'd been divorced two years now, but the lines between us remained hazy and sometimes blurred.

"As your producer *and* your boss *and* your biggest fan, I can assure you this is going to take you to unimaginable heights. This interview will secure your chair on the weekday show," he said. I could practically taste the ambitious flavor of his words.

"I know," I groaned. No one ever aspired to be a weekend anchor. The big stories and the interviews worth watching happened on the weekdays.

"They're *so* close to making their decision." Harrison pinched his fingers together. The network had been quietly discussing my promotion for months, but

Harrison insisted I needed to prove myself a little more before they were willing to replace their beloved Susannah Jethro with a fresh face like myself. "Do you know how many people were scrambling to land Beau Mason's final interview? And he hand picked *you*. *You* of all people. I don't understand your reluctance, Coco. I really don't."

Perhaps it was because I neglected to tell him that Beau and I had a history. One that spanned years. A past defined by young love, dashed hopes, and scar-tissue pain. We were forever tied by an invisible thread and marled an unrequited kind of love that refused to fade away no matter how many years had passed.

Beau Mason's name was a permanent tattoo across my heart, and I was the only one who knew.

"Oh, forgot to tell you that I won't be joining you on this trip," he added. "I've got nothing but meetings all next week, and since you dragged your feet on this interview, I can't reschedule any of them."

I breathed a sigh of relief. Harrison usually accompanied me on all my work trips, but I'd been trying to figure out for the longest time how I was going to explain why I didn't want him to come this time.

"I think I'll survive," I assured him, only a small

part of me knew I was only trying to convince myself.

In every dark night and every lonely moment, my heart always ached for Beau and what might have been. My thoughts scattered in every direction all day long, but in the still, small moments, they always went to him and that burning August night when everything changed.

"Just so we're clear," Harrison said, "it's seven days on Beau's ranch, just the two of you. That was his requirement. You'll get your quotes and material. And I'll work on setting up a time for the crew to go out and film some stills and get some shots of the farm before you do your final sit down interview."

My hand trembled as I gripped my coffee mug and brought it to my lips. I'd interviewed hundreds of people over the span of my career. None of them had that kind of effect of me. The hot liquid scalded my mouth, though I barely felt it, and the second it reached my stomach, it wanted to turn around and come right back.

"I'd like to review your questions before you leave. Make sure you're asking the right questions." He hovered over me, the cadence of his words faster than usual. Of all the interviews he'd booked for me, I'd never seen him so doubtful of my journalistic prowess. "Promise me you're not going to back out of this."

Made in the USA
Lexington, KY
08 April 2015